**THOUGHT CATALOG BOOKS**

# Our Monsters Are Real

# Our Monsters Are Real

## The Pig Man

SEAN SEEBACH

Thought Catalog Books

Brooklyn, NY

**THOUGHT CATALOG BOOKS**

Copyright © 2016 by Sean Seebach

All rights reserved. Published by Thought Catalog Books, a division of The Thought & Expression Co., Williamsburg, Brooklyn. Founded in 2010, Thought Catalog is a website and imprint dedicated to your ideas and stories. We publish fiction and non-fiction from emerging and established writers across all genres. For general information and submissions: manuscripts@thoughtcatalog.com.

First edition, 2016

ISBN 978-0692666142

10 9 8 7 6 5 4 3 2 1

Cover photography by © knape

# Deep Breaths: A foreword by Joel Farrelly

Book forewords are the literary equivalent of elevator music; that benign thing you barely acknowledge on the way to your actual destination and which most people flat-out ignore. Only this time, when those metal doors slide open and they find themselves staring into the darkest recesses of their own unspoken fears and they inevitably start screaming "How? How did he KNOW?", those same people are probably going to regret not taking these final few moments to settle in and brace themselves during my calm before the storm that Mr. Seebach is about to rain on you.

Full Disclosure: Sean and I are buddies and, for that reason, some people might assume this foreword was the result of complete and utter nepotism. And they're probably right but that doesn't really matter because the truth is I wouldn't be Sean's friend if he wasn't a talented writer. That sounded like kind of a dick thing to say. Let me back up…

I first met Sean on the Facebook group that Thought Catalog had set up for its authors to use as a way of networking with each other. Someone on there had asked everybody to post the writers who had influenced us the most, so I posted my list and started scrolling up to some of the previous replies and a few spaces above mine was this guy with almost the exact same answers as me.

The only differences were that I had Richard Matheson

for his novel *I am Legend* as well as his work on the *Twilight Zone* where Sean had listed Joe Hill, another one of my favorite horror writers and a man I greatly respected for his attempt to reboot my other most beloved series, *Tales from the Darkside*. Here's the best part: I had almost included Mr. Hill on my own list but assumed no one would know who he was.

So it should go without saying that Sean and I became fast friends. But you just had to make me say it anyway, didn't you? I hope you're proud of yourself. And you should be because you have great taste in books. The one you're about to read is no exception.

The story starts with the realization of a universal fear, one of those moments of true preternatural dread ingrained in all of us, and it doesn't really let up after that. I had a limited timetable to get this foreword done and had to read most of Sean's book in a single sprint, only to finish it and realize that telling you anymore about *Monsters are Real* would be doing you a great disservice. I considered ending this foreword with a quote from Bioshock but even that would have been too revealing. So instead I'll borrow a line from one of early American cinema's most underrated classics, *Ghostbusters 2*, that accurately describes how I felt during some of *the Pig Man's* more intense moments:

> *Boys? BOYS! You're scaring the straights, okay? Is there anyway we can do this tomorrow?"*

-Dr. Pete Venkman, Scientist

*Joel Farrelly is the author of the viral horror series* Memoirs of a Cam Girl, *currently being adapted into a feature film by Cabin One studios. When Joel isn't waxing knowledgeable about horror, he's usually busy writing it. Mr. Farrelly's work has been featured on Thought Catalog and other prestigious sites such as Cracked.com. He has his own horror novel, titled* Tell Me a Story, *which is also available through Thought Catalog Books.*

# Acknowledgements

*To my wife and son, for allowing me the time to write my bizarre stories. I love you both.*
*To Noelle, Mink, and everyone at Thought Catalog who took a chance with me. Thank You.*
*To M.J. Pack, for your support and all-around tomfoolery. You're a fine writer and a good friend.*
*And to the reader, making all of this possible. Thank you for spending your time with this.*

*I want you to feel like I felt*
*I want you to hurt like I hurt*
*I want you to scream like I screamed*

# 1

The smell of bacon frying in the kitchen woke Penny. She stretched her little arms over her head and released the morning's yawn. She made her way downstairs with her floppy-eared plush bunny, Freddie, dragging her blankie behind her.

She climbed onto a chair and cleared a spot for herself at the kitchen table. Her father, Brad, scraped eggs from the bottom of a skillet. *Sizzle.* Her mother, Diana, sipped a mug of hot black coffee and doodled in the daily paper's puzzle page. *Typical.*

"Hey girlie," Diana said, eyes still on the word jumble.

"Good morning, Mommy!" Penny rubbed her eyes, letting the early morning sun warm her face through the patio door.

"If you want OJ it's in the fridge, pumpkin," Brad said, placing a plate of bacon and scrambled eggs in front of his daughter. "I have to get going."

At eight years old, Penny knew when her parents were fighting. Although they never argued in front of her, they did ignore each other and pretend everything was hunky-dory. Even Penny found this a bit childish.

"I'll be home later tonight, munchkin." Brad kissed Penny's head. She held up Freddie. "Keep an eye on my girls, Fred." He snatched his keys from the table and tugged on Freddie's soft, dangling ear.

"Bye, Daddy." Penny poked at her eggs, waiting for her

mother to say something. Penny wondered if this is what all parents did when they fought, to pretend that each other were invisible.

Diana continued to stare at the paper, moving her pen in a circular motion. After it was clear she would have to be the one to break the silence, Penny went straight for the jugular.

"Why is Daddy mad at you?"

She was good at that, not beating around the bush. Diana knew she got it from her. Penny once called out her kindergarten teacher for mispronouncing the word "orange" (teacher pronounced it *oinge*) and ever since, she was one to get straight to the point. As Penny grew older, she became more inquisitive: "How do babies come from mommy's stomach if the stork brings them?" "How can Santa visit every house in the world in one night?" And (Brad and Diana's favorite) "Why do boys have pickles and I don't?"

Diana knew if she gave her a daughter a bullshit answer, more questions would follow. She placed her pen down and folded her hands, watching Penny swirl a slice of bacon in a pool of ketchup.

"Sometimes…" Diana was careful. "Sometimes, boys can just be silly. Know what I mean pumpkin?"

Penny giggled. "Oh yeah. I know all about that," she said. "Like the time Tommy told everybody at school that I ate a worm and I didn't. It was Tommy who ate that gross worm."

"Yes honey, just like that time."

"Or when Billy pinched me because I could always find him when we played hide-and-go-seek. It's not my fault he's a bad hider, you know?" Penny studiously brushed a lock of hair behind her ear and shoved the bacon into her mouth. "You know Mommy, I've been thinking." Oh no... "We need a Girl's Day. Just you and me."

*Dodged a bullet.*

"I thought you were going to the mall with Madeline and her mom today," Diana said. "You haven't seen her since we moved last month."

"My tummy hurts," Penny said, tucking her upper lip into her bottom lip, pouting. "I'll text her that I don't feel well."

"On whose phone?"

"Yours, of course!"

"Okay. I'll text her mom and tell her that something came up. It isn't nice to lie to your friends."

"Aw, come on! Let me text her! Please?"

*She wants to grow up so fast. And she will, Diana. She'll be sixteen before you know it. Going to dances, boys calling the house... parties. Better enjoy this time while you can.*

Penny stuffed a forkful of scrambled eggs into her mouth and bounced her lower jaw. "See? I'm a chipmunk!" White and yellow rubbery flakes scattered onto Penny's plate.

*Yes. Better enjoy this while you can, Mommy.*

# 2

One of the best things about being an artist, besides being compensated with money to do the thing you love to do (and the occasional day when you can work in your pajamas—okay, that's every day) is the freedom. Part of that freedom means you can go shopping on a weekday afternoon and avoid the weekend shopping crowds, which does make finding a parking place a hell of a lot easier, too.

It also means that a parent shouldn't have to worry about their child being abducted in a crowded area, because, that happens, and it's the most important part of being a parent — to protect your child. This was one of the reasons why the family decided to move to the sleepy town of Edlund, pop. 350. 353 now that The Carters had settled in. They figured it would give Penny the chance to grow up as they did, with down-home-country-values and without the lure of big city influences, like designer drugs and designer friends. It would also give Diana a fresh start, a clean slate, because the city had too many distractions to get any amount of reasonable work done.

They decided to shop at Simply Susan's, a local clothing store for girls and women of all age and size. Penny had the usual stack of sun dresses draped over one arm with matching sandals bundled in the other. She told her mom she was going inside the dressing room to try them on. After some glamour modeling and twirling, Penny had the stack whittled down to four dresses, but insisted she keep all the sandals because they matched the other outfits she had at home. *Our little diva.*

The cashier folded the dresses and tucked them neatly into a recycled brown paper bag. Diana didn't buy anything. She preferred not to dress like the other mothers in town, who looked like they came from a reality show about real housewives. Diana played it simple: slip-on soles, blue jeans, and a comfortable tee shirt. On this day, it was Fleetwood Mac gracing the front, *Rumours Tour*, circa 1977.

"This too, Mommy?" Penny asked, holding up a blue speckled straw hat. Diana removed it from her hand and pulled it snug over Penny's head.

"This too please," Diana said to the cashier. After all, this was a *Girl's Day*.

"Well. Aren't you just the cutest thing?" the cashier said, wrinkling her nose. Penny shifted to a ballerina pose and took a bow toward the cashier.

"How old?" the cashier asked.

"Eight. Going on eighteen!" Diana replied.

"Enjoy it while you can. They grow up fast."

"Trust me, we are!" Penny said.

———————

*We're going to be just fine here.*

They walked down the sidewalk, taking in the vintage red bricked stores, cafés, and antique shops.

"I'm hungry, Momma," Penny said. "What sounds good?"

Diana put her finger to her mouth. "How about…" She spotted a chalkboard sign outside a yogurt shack up ahead. It advertised:

*Vanilla Shakes $5*

*Got the shakes? Add bourbon $10*

"How about ice cream?"

"Yesssss," Penny said. "You read my mind." Then asked "What's bore bon?"

"It's what your father drinks to help him sleep at night."

"In that case I'll have mine without 'cause I don't wanna go to sleep."

"You won't have any because you're eight."

# 3

Penny wiped the melting ice cream off her mother's arm as they drove home on State Route 83. The top was down on the Jeep, a sing-along song was on the radio, and Penny's straw hat was flapping in the wind. A quintessential afternoon for mother and daughter.

"What a horrible idea," Diana said, trying to maintain the integrity of her ice cream cone. "I should've got a shake, like you."

"You should do a lot of things like me," Penny replied as she sucked the thick chocolatey mixture through a straw. She soon placed her hands to her temples.

"Like get a brain freeze?"

Penny rolled her eyes.

"You do that EVERY TIME! Don't worry. It'll pass."

Penny turned down the radio and rubbed her throbbing head. She took in the lush scenic area of forest and pastures and wondered what Madeline and her friends were doing — probably not wishing they hadn't tried to demolish a milk shake in one big gulp. Penny hadn't made any friends yet. She hoped that would change once the school year began in mid-August.

Meanwhile, Diana used her left knee to balance the steering wheel so she could nab a glob of ice cream that silently escaped her cone. It slid down her leg as she reached down to scoop it up. When she did, Penny yelled "Mommy!" Diana glanced up and in a quick flash realized she had veered off the road.

Her instinct jerked the wheel a hard left, which overcompensated the direction the Jeep had gone, causing it to flip over onto the passenger side. The air bags inflated in a *pop!* Followed by a quick *whoosh*. Diana's vision faded, and everything went still.

---

When Diana woke up, she felt disheveled, like she had been crawling around the bottom of a wine bottle. At first she thought maybe she had stayed up too late last night with Brad, hashing out their issues between cocktails, possibly making up (probably not), but when she called Penny's name softly and she didn't respond, Diana suddenly remembered this was real. This was very real.

A sharp pain bolted through Diana's head. It reverberated to the middle of her face. The throbbing reminded her of the low rumbling bass that she would sometimes hear late at night from her dorm room back in her college years.

*Don't freak out, remain calm, Diana. She's probably just stunned from the air bag deploying.*

Diana wrestled around her own air bag, pushing it in different directions, trying to see if her daughter was okay. Diana pulled the keys from the ignition. She extended a small blade from a travel size Swiss army knife on her key ring and punctured the air bags. *Sssssss.*

With the bag out of her way, she found that only the blue speckled beach hat was in the passenger seat. The one she bought Penny only moments ago, when she was safe by her side. Remaining calm was now out of the question.

Diana released the seatbelt while she held the steering wheel so she wouldn't fall. Her hands were slippery from nervous sweat. The smell of fresh earth crowded her nose. She heard bones grinding together when she tried to lift her legs. Her head was dizzy with both physical and emotional pain.

She glanced down toward the brake and accelerator pedals. She could see bone just beneath her skin. It was definitely broken, like when you snap a twig in half over your knee. This made an escape out of the driver's side window now impossible. She grabbed a hold of the seat belt that once held her daughter. The top part was frayed, like someone had chewed through it.

Tears welled up in Diana's eyes, and it wasn't because of the pain that shot through her body like hot electricity. Penny was her sidekick, her daughter, her baby. The thought of her being gone from the wreckage only brought horrible, macabre images that flashed through her mind like a slideshow.

*What if she's mangled in a ball of human bones and flesh in the ditch?*

*What if she was thrown from the vehicle? Her tiny body lying on the road, something for a passing motorist to avoid, or worse, something for the buzzards to enjoy.*

*What if...*

"Penny can you hear me? It's Mommy! I'm okay!" This was a lie but Diana knew she would be okay if she knew Penny was.

*Please God, please. Tell me she just went for help because she couldn't wake me.*

Cicadas sang. The sun reflected off the rim of the Jeep's driver side wheel, which, once spinning, was now still. Diana's adrenaline had run its course and now the only thing that ached, besides her leg, was her heart. Her daughter was gone and Diana was trapped — helpless.

# 4

"How do you expect me to get anything done around here with you on my butt all the time?" blurted Daryl, picking up dirty clothes from his bedroom floor. The statement didn't come out as smooth as he wanted. He stuttered on vowels sometimes whenever he tried to be cute.

"He has what doctors call stunted growth and he need's tutoring because his brain hasn't developed in the way most kids his age has." This was Daryl's mother, Jean, talking into the phone five years ago. Daryl was home-schooled until fourth grade. Jean thought it would be good for him to socialize with kids his own age, make some friends, and get a feel for what it was like to be part of the real world. As if public schooling was any indication of the real world.

He got along fine, now a senior in high school, but he wasn't usually this fussy in the morning. She found him sitting with his legs crossed on his bed comforter, which donned the image of Johnny Cash giving the one finger salute. She hated it.

"Hurry up," Jean said. "Your biscuits are getting cold."

Daryl rolled his eyes. His mother knew what that meant so she let him be. He went to his closet. An array of blue denims and black T-shirts hung neatly in a row along the closet wall. Daryl rubbed his chin, deciding which one to choose from. (They were all the same.) He slipped his legs through a pair, pulled a shirt over his head, and slipped a brown leather belt around his waist. He fastened the belt together with a silver belt buckle, the American flag embroidered in the center. He then pulled a trucker's cap from a shelf and placed it on his head. Too tight. He removed it, adjusted the plastic strap on the back, slapped the inside of the cap with his fist, and pulled it down low over his head.

Daryl took a moment to admire his reflection in the vanity mirror on the wall. He folded the bill of his hat to a perfect curve and tucked a tiny bit of the front part of his shirt into his jeans so he could show off the belt buckle. He then ran his hands over the bill of the trucker's cap, grinned, and slid his right hand from his temple toward his reflection with his index finger extended — a gesture he'd seen used in many westerns.

When Daryl arrived in the kitchen, his father, Frank, was reading The Edlund Dispatch and unlike Diana, Frank didn't doodle in the puzzle page. He was catching up on the Want Ads, looking for any odd jobs he could find since the metal casting company he worked at shut down last spring. Technically, Frank was retired. He pushed a broom at the once productive factory just to pass the time.

"Good Lord, Frank, are you ever going to put that paper down?" Jean said as she put away last night's dishes.

"Is there a crime in liking to keep busy?" Frank said. Noticing Daryl and smirking, he added, "Oh. I see we're going with something new today."

Daryl grimaced and poured hot sauce all over his biscuits and gravy, turning his plate into a molten mountain of lava.

"You ready for a big weekend at the store, son?" Frank said. "The economy still has one foot in the shitter, but I imagine folks will be gearing up for the Fourth. Says here in the Metro that a record year is forecasted for firework sales this year."

Daryl forked the fiery concoction into his mouth. He replied to his dad with a nod, wiped his face off with a cloth towel, and grabbed his keys.

"Gotta go! Don't wanna be late." Daryl said. Jean handed him a steel thermos. "Here honey. Our hard workin' son has to keep his energy up!"

"Thanks, Ma," Daryl said. He kissed his mother on the cheek and exchanged the same gesture he did earlier in the mirror with his dad.

---

Daryl climbed into his pickup truck, a deep red model with white trim that he always kept washed and waxed in the summer. He checked for his harmonica under the driver's seat and placed it in the console. The engine ignited and the low rumble of a small block v8 vibrated his skin. The feeling made Daryl smile every time.

An excited voice with a mid-western twang belted from the speakers when he turned the radio on: "This is Muskrat Matt bringin' you the best of country's outlaws on WKRB, where real country lives."

Daryl turned his volume knob as high as it would go while Dwight Yoakam sang about guitars, Cadillacs, and hillbilly music. He put his left elbow on the driver's side window. His sleeve slid up his stout arm, exposing an impressive farmer's tan — the kind of tan you only get by working outdoors under the summer sun—and headed to his place of employment, Jimbo's Market & General Store.

# 5

The market was packed full of people trying to beat the procrastinating Fourth of July shoppers. The cold air instantly turned Daryl's sweat into cool, soothing drops of heaven.

"Register seven needs a hand, D," said Jimbo. (Only Daryl's friends had the privilege of calling him D. He was Daryl to everybody else.) Jimbo's blue tie was in disarray against his disheveled white collared shirt that covered his bloated belly. His brown pants were also wrinkled from hustling about, trying to meet his customer's needs. He patted Daryl on the back as he passed him, tapping rolled up inventory sheets against his hip as he did.

"Boy am I glad to see you, D. It's going to be a wild one this weekend. I hope you ate your Wheaties this morning!"

Daryl started to have second thoughts about drowning his breakfast with pepper sauce. His stomach was like a life raft lost at sea, and he knew it wasn't just the spices turning his stomach over. Samantha worked register seven and had been ever since she was hired. She walked the stage last year, got her diploma, and was now attending college in-state. She needed a job in the summer for extra cash, Jimbo needed a cashier, and voila! There she was. She had her dirty blonde hair in a bun today, exposing her neck to the cool air that blew from the vent above register seven. Her legs were long and firm. Her skin tan, the same golden brown as Daryl's arms, and complimented her blue-flecked eyes. It wasn't just his breakfast that upset his stomach. Those eyes made it feel funny every time he saw them.

"Yay, Daryl's here!" Samantha said, meeting his stare.

Daryl's felt his cheeks burn a little as he lifted a bag of charcoal into a shopping cart.

"Don't squish my buns young man," said the old lady at the register. "I'm having a barbecue and I can't be serving hot dogs and hamburgers with squished buns!" The irritable woman gave Samantha a stack of coupons as she made her demands to Daryl.

"I never squish buns on the job, ma'am," Daryl said, making Samantha turn her head and snort. Daryl loved to make Samantha laugh. Another success.

# 6

After his shift at the market, Daryl drove down the back roads to his grandpa's farm. Hazy humidity hung above the acres of land when he arrived. He signaled to Gramps that he was ready. Bales of hay came rolling toward Daryl as he locked his meaty hands, protected with thick leather gloves, into the metal wire that bounded each bale of hay. They reminded him of shredded wheat cereal as he stacked them. A cereal that he could no longer enjoy since he became old enough to bale.

The back of Daryl's neck began to turn purple, a ripe beet, as the fiery sun pickled his skin. It was so hot that sweat seemed to evaporate before any moderate breeze had the chance to cool it.

Grandpa Woody decided to call it a day around dusk. He couldn't work as long as he used to since his heart attack last year. The doc said he needed to take it easy, but he had more to teach Daryl about farming: the inner workings of the tractor for when it malfunctioned for instance, and what to do when the well on the property flooded. Woody needed to remain healthy until Daryl was ready to take over the farm. He supposed then he could go full tilt until his heart finally gave out. What do doctors know about health anyway?

Woody came out from inside the house holding a pitcher of iced tea and two glasses. Lemon slices battled each other for the surface as he eased into his oak rocking chair. Soon the bullfrogs could be heard croaking at one another. But for now, it was the sound of cicadas echoing through the fields of tall grass.

The tea felt good against Daryl's hot throat, quenching the kind of thirst only hard farming work can produce. Daryl poured himself a second glass of the sweet elixir, ignoring the splatter caused by the ice and lemon slices as they toppled over one another, *blop-clank-blop*. He took a generous sip from his glass, eased his trucker's cap to the crown of his head, and wiped the summer sweat from his face—grinding the salt that accumulated on his skin between his fingers.

They sat there together on the front porch. The porch that Woody built for his deceased wife, and watched the crimson sun sink below the horizon.

# 7

Summer break for most students meant returning home to flip hotcakes or work odd construction jobs that paid under the table. For Brad, it meant cooking pizzas for the campus locals at a pizzeria while he took advanced writing courses through August. And that was where he met Diana.

She was carrying a Bukowski paperback, either Bar Fly or Post Office, he couldn't remember. What he did remember was that she looked stunning even though she wasn't wearing any makeup, which accentuated her glowing face, devoid of any blemishes. Her dark hair was pinned up in a ponytail. She wore sneakers without socks and had a University pullover that hung low over her yoga pants. A natural beauty.

"Are you still open?" Diana asked.

Brad was stacking a pile of to-go menus by the register when he looked up at her. His heart skipped for a moment. "For like, five more minutes."

"Great!" she said. "Can I get a medium pepperoni please?"

"Sure. That'll be ten-fifty," Brad replied.

Diana put the book down on the counter and searched the front pocket of her pullover. Her hand came out empty on the other side. Showing a bit of vulnerability, she frantically searched her handbag: a cloth turquoise pouch that hung from her shoulder.

"I'll get it in the oven," Brad said. A girl that pretty had to come from money. She's going to ask to use the restaurant's phone to call Daddy and he will give her a series of numbers to pay for the pizza. Then, Daddy will immediately cancel her credit card and have a new one sent to her by the following afternoon so she can put gas in her imported car, go shopping for things no college student should rightfully buy, and do other things that young adults who come from money do.

Diana found herself alone in the restaurant. The jukebox was unplugged and the chairs were overturned on the tabletops. Brad returned with her pizza moments later. The lights were dimmed above his face and hers. It was kind of romantic.

"That'll be…"

"Yeah. Ten-fifty. I know."

"Whoa, I'm not trying to…if you need to use the phone…"

"Shit." Diana dug through her handbag. "No, I don't need to use the phone." She locked eyes with Brad. He froze. He hadn't realized until now how beautiful her eyes were behind her long lashes. His stomach fluttered, like he was on the peak of a canyon, looking over the edge to a seemingly bottomless descent.

She sighed. "I just forgot to cash my check from the bookstore. I've been so busy with work and class that it slipped my mind."

*She isn't a trust fund brat. Interesting. I might have a chance with this one.*

"What are you studying?" Brad asked.

"I major in art. Look, I can scrape up the money back at my dorm. It's only half a block away."

Brad folded his arms, feeling like he had the upper hand in the conversation.

"I tell you what. How about I give you this pizza? If you show me your stuff." Diana scrunched her face, her head tilted to one side.

"I mean your art," Brad said. "If you show me your ART."

Diana blushed. *Nice Brad, you almost lost her.* Nobody had ever asked to see her art before, at least not with genuine interest. Sure she knew he was trying to score a date, albeit a poor attempt, but who was to say she wasn't either.

"Okay, deal." She reached over the counter to shake his hand. He gently held her fingers and shook them.

She reluctantly took the pizza from Brad and before she left, said: "Are you sure you won't get in any trouble for giving me this?"

"Nah. I get a free pizza every shift. Besides, I might spew if I have to eat another pizza again, free or not!" He placed his hands around his neck like he was choking.

"Okay, Romeo. Meet me in front of the bookstore at ten o'clock tomorrow morning."

"I'll be there." Brad said, following her with his eyes as she left. He removed his apron and tossed it into the laundry bag. "He shoots, he scores!"

He pumped his fists as he locked the front door. He returned to the counter to count down the cash register and noticed Diana left her book. Scrambling to the window, Brad peeked through the blinds. She was within shouting distance, but he let her go. He'd return the book tomorrow. What better way to break the ice on a first date than by talking about a famed author?

And it worked. Brad and Diana began dating that summer and never looked back. They were married the following year after they graduated, moved to the city, and began building their life together. However, that life was already teetering on destruction — and was about to come crumbling down.

# 8

"You must think I'm a complete lunatic," Brad said to the librarian. Her name, Leslie, was etched into a plastic name tag that was pinned to her left, sagging breast.

"A lunatic? Maybe." Leslie said. "A *complete* lunatic? No. That's my ex-husband."

"I'm actually doing research for a crime novel I'm writing." He leaned over the counter and placed an open hand to the corner of his mouth and whispered: "It's about a serial killer." He winked at Leslie. Unimpressed, she pushed her glasses up the bridge of her nose.

"These are due back in two weeks," she said. "The fee is a dollar for each day they're late."

Brad offered her a smile, hoping to get one in return. He didn't.

Returning to his car, Brad balanced the stack of books in one hand while he turned his phone off silent. Good library etiquette.

He had a voice message from an unknown caller. Maybe it was from his wife's lover, back in New York. Maybe he was calling to apologize for fucking his wife, to say that he didn't know she was married, to say that it was only the one time. Brad wasn't in the mood to listen to a man pleading for forgiveness, but the area code was local, so he figured he'd listen to it.

"I assume this is the husband of Diana Carter," the female

voice said. "I searched her phone and dialed the contact stored as 'Husband'. My name is Sally Pruit and I'm the head nurse at Edlund Medical Center. Please call us back at the following number. It concerns your wife…"

Brad stopped the message and immediately dialed the number back while he punched in Edlund Medical Center into his GPS.

*Maybe she really did it this time. Maybe she finally offed herself. All that guilt from infidelity has finally worn her conscious.*

His thoughts quickly shifted to when Diana sold her first painting. All those lustful eyes from thin, hipster men wearing horn-rimmed glasses, complimenting her work, her gown and her body. She liked the attention and Brad knew it from the way she would brush her hair back over her shoulder and smile. It was the same gesture she used before he kissed her for the first time; under the lonely street lamp in front of the college bookstore, after their first date.

*What about Penny? She was with Madeline at the mall. Thank God she wasn't with Diana. How would he tell her? She would never be able to get over seeing her mother sprawled out on the bathroom floor, perhaps laying in a pool of her own blood as it poured from her open wrists. Or maybe it was the lesser of the evils. An overdose from mixing wine with painkillers that only helped her function at this point in her life. The big deep sleep to end all nightmares.*

Brad continued his way through afternoon traffic, stopping at every yellow light and taking extra time to completely stop at every red, octagon sign. He was now in no hurry to find out what happened to Diana. His heart ached, a pendulum swinging from anger to sadness, and all he could think about was his daughter.

# 9

Penny's eyes adjusted to a concrete room. It smelled of wet, dirty laundry. Rusty farm equipment hung sporadically from moss covered walls. Fresh blood formed a puddle below a pointed sickle. It's crescent blade and curved handle was worn and faded.

She was scared. Her knees were scraped and she had dark purple bruises under each arm. She removed chunks of dirt and grass from her hair as she could only recall the blurry image of the road when the jeep made a 90-degree flip into the field. It reminded her of being on a roller coaster during the corkscrew turn. *Mommy and I were in an accident.*

A silver water dish sat by a wooden staircase that led to a door. A yellow beam of light glowed under the one inch gap where the lip of the top step met the ground floor. Shadows from footsteps danced below the doorway, causing a strobe-effect on the staircase.

Penny rubbed her eyes to discover that her wrists were bound together with a rough twine. She felt a heavy weight around her waist as she crawled toward the water dish. This was caused by a coiled chain secured by a cinder block. The chain dragged along the cold, concrete floor. Its links ground together, making this simple task seem impossible.

Foot by foot, she slowly made her way to the water. Her distorted reflection stared back at her, making the bloody scrapes on her face wiggle. With both hands only inches apart, she managed to pour some of the rotten, egg-smelling water into her mouth.

There was mumbling behind the door. She crawled over to a pile of feed sacks and laid her aching head down. She knew she was in danger. She knew she had to dial emergency, 911, just like she was taught in school. And she knew the people upstairs weren't going to let her. Penny began to cry.

# 10

Although a cheap model, Daryl's harmonica made him feel important. It was the only thing he found he could do naturally. He couldn't throw a perfect spiral or sink a free throw to save his life, but boy could he get down on that harmonica. It was also the only thing Daryl had ever won.

---

Daryl earned the prize last year when the carnival came to town. He was successful in sending an iron piston into a large, rusty bell that was placed on top of a column. The column reminded him of a thermometer big enough for King Kong.

"Hot damn, we have a winner!" the carnie said after Daryl made the old bell ring-a-ding-a-ling. Lights exploded and buzzers when off in a frenzy. Daryl dropped the rubber mallet to the ground and flexed his muscles, showing off his twelve-inch pythons.

"Over-stuffed teddy bears don't seem appropriate for a young man such as yourself," said the carnie, carefully caressing his pencil-thin mustache. He wore a multi-colored jacket that had homemade patchwork over each lapel. His brown leather boots were faded and worn so much that a socked toe poked out of the one on his right foot.

"Care to choose from The Great Mystery Box?" asked the carnie. He handed Daryl a black, wooden box. A purple question mark inside quotations was painted on the front.

Daryl remembered the box being very light and when he dug his hand down through the cloth covered hole, it seemed to have no bottom or sides, like infinite space.

Daryl's arm was elbow deep when the carnie's concerned eyes met his. He eased Daryl's arm back and through his megaphone said: "Easy partner! Ain't no gold in them thar hills!"

Unnoticed, a crowd gathered around Daryl. They cheered at the Carnie's statement and that's when Daryl pulled out his prize: a shiny, steel harmonica. It was the most precious thing he ever held. Daryl held it high for all to see.

"Do you play?" the carnie asked.

Daryl shook his head.

"Well it's never too late to learn! Let's give Marietta's, I mean Edlund's, strongest man a round of applause!"

Whistles shot through the cheering crowd. The carnie eased into Daryl like an affectionate cat wanting attention. He smelled of alcohol and sweet cherry pipe tobacco.

"The box chose your prize, and like I said…it's never too late to learn."

––––––––––––––

That statement stuck with Daryl and he started playing it right away. He caught on fast, teaching himself twelve-bar blues and tongue blocking techniques from books he checked out at the library. Not soon after, he moved on to more advanced playing, like train whistles and chord bends.

Then Daryl was introduced, by his Grandpa Woody, to the album that would change his life forever, Nebraska by Bruce Springsteen. Daryl appreciated the way The Boss was able to tell stories through song. He was even more appreciative of the record when he learned that Springsteen made it on an eight-track recorder in his bedroom.

"Johnny 99" was his favorite, mostly for the harmonica riffs. It didn't take long before he was playing each part with The Boss, tearing through each section with precision and harmonizing with each note.

Daryl moved on to Bruce Springsteen & The E Street Band Live/1975-85. He came to realize the songs they wrote were about, and for, the hard working class of America. These were the same people he grew up with. The people he saw every day at Jimbo's Market. The people who made an honest living with their sleeves rolled up and smiles on their faces. He would drum his fingers to Max Weinberg's steady back beats. He got chills from Clarence Clemons' sax solos which, on songs like 'Badlands', sounded like an angel reigning down from the heavens to save all sinners.

———————

Because Daryl was able to hang with The E Street Band on record, he had the confidence to think he could also hang with a live band. The next morning after helping his Grandpa bale hay, he decided to take the long way home. He saw a portable road sign on a gravel parking lot with interchangeable lettering that advertised:

BLUES FRIDAY NITES
$1 DRAFTS TIL 9

It was still early in the afternoon, so the arrow above the sign that pointed to the tavern wasn't flashing.

A hazy fog from cigarette smoke hung above two billiard

tables to the left when Daryl entered the tavern. Panning to the right, he saw a small stage erected in front of a tiled dance floor. Stains from sweat and whiskey were prominent between the tiles' black and white checkered squares. Two small amplifiers sat to the back of the stage. In the middle stood a tall microphone stand with guitar picks notched into the side. A dominant POW/MIA flag served as the stage backdrop.

Daryl took all of this in, just before the spring-loaded front door smacked him in his ass. This drew the attention of the two men behind the bar, who were counting liquor inventory. They both wore open leather vests, exposing cheap tattoos over their chest and abdomen. The one holding a pen and clipboard spoke first:

"We're closed," he said. "Open at four."

Daryl blinked his eyes, unsure of how to respond.

"He said we're closed, chief," the other man said, holding up a bottle of vodka to the dim light, ignoring Daryl.

*Are you gonna say something? This is your chance, man. Just say something…*

"Says outside you play blues," Daryl finally said. "On Friday."

The men gave their full, aggravated attention to Daryl.

"Um…I play the blues," Daryl said and removed the harmonica from the back pocket of his jeans, holding it up high to show he meant business.

"You don't say," said the man, putting a bottle of vodka down and placing it back on the shelf. "Well, it just so happens we've been lookin' for a harp sucker. C'mon over here and let's hear what you got."

Daryl's confident expression turned to a whole hearted grin as he eased his way toward the bar. He was nervous, but he felt safe. The bar offered a comforting barrier between him and the two men.

The man holding the clipboard pulled out a cigarette and extended his arm. "Name's Jud. And this here's Scooter."

Daryl shook Jud's hand with a sweaty palm. Scooter formed a fist and Daryl bumped it with his own.

"Nice tatt," Daryl said, breaking his nervousness. He was referring to the serpent on Jud's hand. It was coiled, mouth open, exposing two fangs and a forked tongue.

"Don't tread on me," Daryl said. Jud's incredulous look made Daryl feel proud that he knew the reference.

"Yeah, that's right. There ain't enough room on my hand for all them words so I figured to just get the symbol. I was blessed with long fingers for the guitar (he pronounced it gee-tar and wiggled his tall digits). And they ain't let me down yet."

"Well, what are you waiting for, young man?" Scooter said. "Wail on that piece already." Scooter helped himself to a cigarette from Jud's pack and folded his arms. Daryl removed a camouflage handkerchief from his other back pocket and wiped the sweat from his hands.

"You-you have any water?" Daryl asked.

Jud reached below the bar and presented Daryl with a bottle of spring water. He drank from it, emptying half the bottle down his throat.

"Thanks," Daryl said. Jud and Scooter snickered at each other, picking up on Daryl's nervousness.

Daryl put the harmonica to his lips. Playing in the key of 'G', he started out slow to warm up his lungs. He progressed through the one, four, and five chords with precision. Jud blew a cloud of smoke towards the ceiling fan above them and placed his cigarette in a plastic ashtray. Scooter did the same. They nodded their heads and tapped their hands on the bar top in time with the harmonica.

Sweat beaded from Daryl's forehead as he picked up the pace. He felt a powerful surge flow through his body and the notes he was playing began to bend. The harmonica started to glow, an ochre hue. And although he felt euphoric, that he was on the path to something great, Daryl no longer controlled his breathing.

He played louder, faster. He ran through the twelve-bar blues like a prodigy. An intense heat radiated from the harmonica. It became so hot, Daryl thought his lips would blister if he continued. But he kept going, stomping his foot as he crouched over, circling in pace. His hands flailed over his mouth as he released each chord, note for note.

"Okay, okay," Jud said.

Daryl continued. Jud cupped his hands over his mouth and raised his voice:

"I said that's good! You can stop now!"

Daryl let the final note ring and echo through the empty tavern. The harmonica ceased to glow and quickly returned to its original metallic color. Scooter handed Daryl a bar towel so he could wipe the dripping sweat from his face.

"I'd say we have ourselves a real whammer jammer here Scooter!" Jud said. "How old are you, son?

Daryl straightened his back and stuck his chest out, trying to look mature.

"Eighteen, sir."

"Have you ever played with a band before?" Jud asked.

Daryl hung his head.

"Then come back tomorrow around six. We'll jam a bit. If you gel with the band, rather, if we gel with YOU, you can gig with us. Band goes on at seven-thirty. We usually play until midnight."

Daryl thanked them. He couldn't wait to tell Samantha the good news.

# 11

Daryl pulled into Jimbo's parking lot just as his engine stalled. He coasted his truck into a vacant parking space, right next to a shopping cart corral. The radio went south. It flickered on and off for a moment, then nothing. Daryl's trustworthy classic '78 pick-up truck was dead.

He popped the hood and checked the spark plugs. Grandpa Woody said it was the first thing you did when a vehicle died, next to making sure it had gas. The plugs seemed fine, but one was a little loose, so Daryl secured it and turned the key. Again, nothing.

"Need a hand, D?" Jimbo said, while pushing shopping carts across the parking lot. His jovial belly bounced behind a green smock. The words 'Jimbo's Market' were etched in white above two oversized pockets.

"It just died on me," Daryl said. "I don't know what's wrong. It has gas and the plugs are fine."

Jimbo sat behind the steering wheel and turned the key, the same act Daryl had done just moments ago. Looking around, he inspected the instrument panel.

"Yup. It's dead alright. Could be one of two things: bad alternator or the battery's gone kaput. Either way, it's an easy fix. Sit tight. The battery might just need a charge."

Jimbo arrived moments later in an '88 Buick. It had original paint—no dents, scratches, or dings, as if he just drove it off the showroom floor. He raised the hood, revealing an immaculate engine. He placed a red claw to the positive ends of both batteries and a black claw to the negative ends.

"I'm going to let my car run. Give it about five minutes. I'll be right back, D."

"Thank you, sir," Daryl said. Jimbo's face was covered in thick sweat. Another scorcher.

"Don't mention it. One good thing about these old trucks…they're easy to work on. We'll get you rolling again in no time."

Daryl leaned against his truck and rested his head on his forearm. He watched as his own sweat poured down over the black pavement. *Splunk!* He adjusted his position, trying to make the sweat land in consecutive places while he thought about what just happened at the Elkhorn.

He knew he was good, but to play with a band, in a room full of strangers was something entirely new. Was he ready? And what if he lost control of his harmonica again? Daryl figured it happened to anyone who was in the proverbial 'zone'. Or maybe he just imagined it. Either way, Daryl chalked it up as adrenaline. Adrenaline and nerves.

"Hey good lookin'," Samantha said. "Need a ride?"

Daryl lifted his head and found Samantha unlocking her Volkswagen Beetle. There was a large peace sign stuck to the rear tinted window. The Beetle's lemon-yellow color matched her personality — bright, warm, joyful.

"No. Jimbo and I have everything under control. He thinks it's the battery or alternator."

"The alterna-what?" Samantha said, giving Daryl a sarcastic smile. Her dimples made her look five years younger, as if that was possible. She was only nineteen. She stuck the tip of her tongue out between her teeth and shielded the brutal sun from her eyes with her hand.

"The alternator," he said. "Mechanic's jargon for a generator."

"Oh sure, okay," she replied, rolling her eyes. "Care to keep me company while my car cools down?"

Daryl smiled and joined her. A rush of vanilla scented air filled his nose when he sat down.

"Sure is nice in here," Daryl said, a little nervous. "Do you always keep your car this clean?"

"Yeah. I try to. I haven't had to haul my nieces around in a while." Samantha giggled, a little nervous herself. "My back seat turns into their toy chest." She angled the air vents towards Daryl. A cool rush of air hit his face.

"Mind if I play some music while we wait for Jimbo?"

"Sure I do. I mean, no, I don't mind."

She turned on her car stereo. Garth Brooks was singing about having friends in low places. "Oh my God, I love this song!" she said, turning up the volume. She sang along with the chorus. She was out of key, but Daryl didn't mind. He was just happy to be this close to her. A girl that pretty can get away with singing out of key. The combination of vanilla, her sweat, and the cool air made him feel a bit uneasy. He wiped his palms on his jeans, hoping she wouldn't notice.

"My sister and I saw him last summer at The Coliseum," she said. "It was the best concert I've ever been to." Then she placed her arm over the head rest of the passenger seat and turned into him.

"How about you? Have you ever been to a concert, Daryl?"

Daryl crossed his feet and placed his hands under his legs. "No, but I'd like to sometime."

"You should. They're so much fun. I just loooove music!"

*This is it. The perfect opportunity to ask her.*

"Well, um, what are you doing Friday night?" he asked, staring through the windshield.

"I don't have any plans really. Why?"

"I'm in this band...I mean, I might be playing at this place called The Elkhorn Tavern. I have an audition."

"That's great!"

"It's blues stuff. Starts around seven-thirty."

He finally had the courage to look at her. Samantha's eyes bounced up and down. She looked away, then back at him.

"Would you like to come and check us out?" he said.

Samantha pulled her arm back and adjusted herself in her seat, a matter-of-fact position.

"That depends," she said smiling. "What do you play?"

"This old thing," he said and removed the harmonica from his pocket.

"Can I see it?" she said, taking it from his hand. She placed the harmonica to her thin lips and blew. It didn't make a sound. She tried again, nothing, then handed it back. "Does it work?"

"Yeah, I mean, it does when I play it. Maybe you're doing it wrong." He returned the harmonica back to his pocket. "So what do you say?"

She leaned further away and pressed her body against the driver's side door. She smiled, exposing those youthful dimples again.

"I'd love to. Only with one condition, though. I have to

bring a friend. I don't want to be by myself in a rowdy roadhouse bar on a Friday night alone."

"Is this friend a…"

"A guy? Oh, no. Do you remember Kelly Franklin? She graduated with me last year."

"Oh yeah, sure. She's nice."

"She's a little wild, I know, but we've been friends ever since I can remember."

"Hey, D!" Jimbo said, tapping on the window. Daryl jumped. He was so locked into his conversation with Samantha that he had completely forgotten about his truck.

"C'mon out. It was the battery. Got your truck running like a marathon!"

Daryl opened the door. A rush of festering heat pounded his face. He poked his head inside. "See you Friday?"

"You got it," Samantha said, giving him a wink.

"You working on a date in there?" Jimbo asked.

"No, sir. Just friends."

"Whatever you say, buddy," Jimbo said, laughing as he wiped black grime off his hands with the green smock.

"The battery was ninety bucks, but since you worked over last week…no charge."

"Are you sure?"

"Aw hell D, you'd do the same for me."

Daryl closed the hood to his truck. Jimbo leaned into him.

"Take this from someone who knows. The prettier they are, the harder you'll fall. Don't put all your eggs in one basket, D. You're still young. Know what I mean?"

Daryl knew what he meant but that wasn't going to stop him from going "all in" with the girl who had his heart.

Summertime romance can make someone blind to obvious warnings. Samantha, however, didn't possess any of those. At least none that he could tell. For one, she loved music. Two, she dug his kind of music, and three, well, she was a fox. A perfect Ten! And he knew if he ever had the chance to impress her, rockin' out with a blues band would be it.

# 12

Final day of school. Instead of spending his time studying, which is what you're supposed to do in study hall, Daryl spent it thinking of Samantha. The way she would turn her shoulder as he approached her register; ice frosted teeth packed tightly together, deep, infinite eyes, the way her hair would just flow freely across her shoulder. Her chin a perfect little curve below her jaw. Her posture making sure everything below the neck was in place. He played with the harmonica, pushing it in and out of his pocket while he counted down the minutes until lunch time.

---

The lunch bell rang. The cafeteria was crowded with pimple-faced freshmen, pubescent facial-haired seniors, and all the other outcasts, smarty pants, athletes, and divas that make up a student body. Daryl was starving. He could not wait to shovel today's featured menu item into his face: The ever popular 'haystack taco.' 'The Stack,' as the students referred to it, was composed of mystery taco meat, shredded cheese, lettuce, and tomato, all heaped over a bed of corn chips. The Stack was better going in, then it was coming out, but no one seemed to mind as they demanded More salsa! More salsa! on top of this marvelous creation.

Fortunately for Daryl, he always carried a bottle of hot sauce when The Stack was served. He didn't care too much for the public school version of salsa. It was watered down by the cafeteria staff in order to "stretch it out".

The line was still considerably long when Daryl took his place. He was behind two cheerleaders. They were jabbering about someone who apparently took a shit in somebody's backpack during second period.

"It was so gross," said the one with a blonde ponytail. "I heard the janitor was out of gloves so he had to wipe the backpack out with his bare hands!"

They giggled and whispered some more nonsense about boys and making out behind the bleachers during gym class. Somebody had their period and clogged up the toiled with a soiled tampon. Typical dumb shit.

Just when the line started moving forward, three seniors and a junior squeezed themselves in front of Daryl, ignoring the unwritten law that seniors don't ditch fellow seniors (neither do underclassmen.)

"Sup, farm boy?" said Sid, the leader of The Gruesome Foursome. He was considered the nastiest kid in school. He was your typical teenager with an identity crisis. A ridiculous gold chain drooped around his neck. He wore a neon-blue baseball hat that was purposely tilted to one side. A transparent mustache wrapped around his upper lip, a flawed attempt to look older. Daryl wondered what Sid would dress like if MTV didn't exist.

It was rumored that Sid slept with the home economics teacher, Ms. Gretchen. None of this was of course proven but everyone found it convenient that she resigned from her position shortly after word got out that Sid did the deed. Ms. Gretchen was the youngest of the teacher faculty, who wore skirts that came just below her ass and blouses that accentuated her round, perky breasts. She was the stereotypical "hot for teacher" type. The one teacher every student would love to have a lesson with after class. Daryl figured she moved to Florida, where most people go when they need to run from something. He imagined her teaching high school in a room with no air conditioning, speaking in a new Southern drawl, distracting the boys in the hallways. Either way, the rumor just added to Sid's bad boy legacy.

"Something funny?" Sid said. "Why you smiling at me like some queer?"

"I'm not smiling," Daryl replied, looking beyond Sid and his band of bullies, trying to put his focus on the food pyramid poster hanging by the exit door.

Students began passing the blockage created by them. Each time Daryl tried to move ahead in line, Sid would step in front of Daryl, blocking him from moving forward, as if he had to solve a riddle from a troll that guarded a bridge.

"What you going to do now, sheep fucker?" Sid said, sizing Daryl up with infuriating eyes.

"You forgot to take the sticker off your hat," Daryl said, referring to the hologram square stuck on the underside of Sid's bill.

"That's my style, bumpkin," Sid said, stepping in closer to Daryl. Daryl could smell stale smoke on his breath.

Feeling the tension, heads began turning toward Daryl, anticipating a good old-fashioned lunch room brawl. And that's when Sid shoved Daryl into Flint, Sid's partner in hazing. Flint was a skinny kid with bad acne. He too, smelled of the same cheap cigarettes as Sid. He grabbed Daryl by his shoulder and snatched the harmonica from his back pocket.

"Hey! Hey! Look here boys," Flint said. "Daryl's a man of constant sorrow!"

"Give it back," Daryl warned. "I'm only going to tell you once."

"Or what?" Sid said. He pointed a dirty fingernail in Daryl's face. "What-are-you-going-to-do-about-it?" Then he flicked that dirty fingernail into Daryl's nose.

Daryl slapped Sid's hand away from his face with his left hand and formed a fist with his right.

"Do it, sheep fucker. I fucking dare ya."

Just before Daryl could unload on Sid's pointed nose, Mr. Jeffries, the gym teacher and varsity basketball coach, approached them from behind the lunch line.

"What's going on here?" he inquired. Part sarcastic, part serious.

"Nothing sir," Flint said. "I was just showing Daryl here my new harmonica. Nice and shiny ain't it?"

"Ain't isn't a word," said Mr. Jeffries. "And Sid, if you're planning on graduating this year and playing Division III basketball, I suggest you don't skip your afternoon classes today. You can't afford another absence, or detention."

Nodding his head, Sid looked at Daryl. "You got it, coach."

Daryl watched as The Gruesome Foursome approached the lunch counter. Flint looked back at Daryl and smiled as he slid Daryl's harmonica into his pocket.

"It was nice of you to let those boys in front of you, Daryl," Mr. Jeffries said. "Look, I know everyone is on edge because it's the last day of school and it's not ideal that we had to make up these days after the horrible winter we had. But that doesn't give you the right to take it out on my point guard. Got it?"

Daryl nodded.

"Now get up there and get some lunch before it's all gone. I hear they're serving haystacks today!" Mr. Jeffries smirked at Daryl and flirtatiously walked over to a group of girls, who also happened to be cheerleaders, by the pop machine. Daryl heard the girls giggle as Mr. Jeffries teased them about their hair.

By the time he made it to the counter, the only thing left was the runny salsa. Daryl settled on a bag of chips from the vending machine. He sat by himself, as he always did, crunching each salty oval one by one. He let each chip sit on his tongue until it burned while he thought of a way to get his harmonica back.

# 13

That night in his bedroom, Daryl skimmed through Country Music Monthly, a magazine that featured new country acts from across America. He didn't care too much for what people today considered country, but picked this issue up particularly for the Top 100 Country songs of all-time list. Hank Williams Jr. didn't even crack the Top Ten.

"Bullshit politics," he said and threw the magazine into his bedroom wall which was decorated with posters of muscle cars, tractors, and various hunting game.

Daryl wasn't surprised by how Mr. Jeffries handled the situation at school. No matter what, teacher-coaches always favor the athlete, especially in a small town where sports are more important to the community and faculty than academics. Never mind. Daryl was still fuming about the harmonica. Not only was his audition tomorrow but he already invited Samantha to come. And it wasn't like he didn't blow the socks off Jud and Scooter, so he knew there was a strong chance he'd make the band. But none of that mattered if he didn't have his instrument.

"Is everything okay?" Jean said, cracking Daryl's bedroom door. "I thought I heard something fall."

"It was nothing."

She rested her head against the door jamb, drying her hands off with her apron. Little roosters danced around a big red barn as she ruffled the fabric through her hands.

"Most kids are happy when school is over," she said, "for good."

"I'm fine, ma."

"Okay, sweetie. Dinner is ready if you're hungry."

Daryl stretched himself out, making sure he cracked his joints and knuckles together.

"I'm just tired is all," he said. "I'll be down later."

Jean smiled at her son, soon to be graduated. *Where did the time go? One day you're changing their diapers and reading them their favorite bedtime stories, next they're asking for the car keys and looking for work.* She left him alone and closed the door behind her.

Before Daryl fell asleep, he thought of Samantha. They were together in a hay loft, caressing each other's face and kissing each other in a subtle way. It was a comforting fantasy before drifting off. But that's not what he dreamt about.

---

The red sun was beginning to set behind a steel paneled silo, turning the sky into a vast purple sea. Daryl reached for the sunglasses that rested on top of his head to shield his eyes from the final moments of daylight. What he felt instead was a withering cord that coiled around his wrists. The pulsing tube, moist and warm, squeezed against his skin. Rapid strokes of a ribbon-like material tickled his neck. The sky grew darker and the air more humid, making every breath more suffocating than the last.

Daryl titled his head and removed the obstruction. It was a serpent. It gazed at him in dominance with placid eyes, lowering its mouth like a drawbridge. Identical fangs emerged from inside the serpent's hourglass jaw. Sharp and ready to strike. Its forked tongue danced between the two fangs while the tip of its tail slowly vibrated.

He uncoiled the serpent and pulled it taut. He turned it over. On its belly were the words 'Don't Tread On Me', written in gothic lettering. He put the serpent on the ground and it zig-zagged its way into the foggy darkness.

The moon was suddenly visible. Full and bright, it provided him with enough light to move forward. Daryl could hear the gravel crunch under his cowboy boots as he carefully waded through the fog.

Up ahead was a corral. Inside the corral were pigs. Angry pigs. They stomped and snorted around each other like they were waiting for him. A girl's laughter echoed in the distance through the haze. Daryl approached the corral and placed his hands around the metal gate to peek inside. The pigs were gone, but the snorting and stomping sounds were still there. The corral began to vibrate. He fell back and waved his arms in a circular motion to keep from falling. The disgusting scent of pig shit filled his nose. From the opposite direction came another burst of laughter.

"Who's there?" Daryl said. He began walking around the corral, one careful boot in front of the other. Another giggle was followed by a scream. A line of warm urine filled his chaps.

"Pee pants! Pee pants!" The girl's voice said, mocking him. Daryl shut his eyes and tried to wake up. It was as if he was hovering only inches from the ground. When he opened his eyes, a little girl stood in front of him. She had on a formal dress, like something one would wear to church or a birthday party. Her hair was tied up in pigtails. She was barefoot and her knees were scraped. She looked exhausted and afraid and was holding Daryl's harmonica.

"I can play anything on this," she said. "I didn't even have to practice. Wanna see?" The words slipped out of her mouth like a dare.

Daryl reached for his harmonica and although the girl was only a few feet in front of him, it felt like he was still miles away from her. Time and space were non-existent. She blew into the shiny bar. A hollow C Note hung in the suspended fog and caused the corral to shake violently. Just like that, the corral was full of mad, dirty pigs. The volatile grunting became distorted, like the sound was projected through an oscillating fan, spreading in every direction. Their snouts were black from dried blood as they trampled over each other, trying to be the first to get a taste of Daryl and the little girl.

She grabbed him by the hand and they both ran. They ran fast and hard through the heavy air.

"I want my Mommy and Daddy," she said. "Do you know where they're at?" She kept pleading with him. "Where are they? Where, where, WHERE?!"

Daryl sat up and found himself mummified in his Man in Black comforter. He untangled himself and checked his crotch. It was dry. It was five-thirty in the morning. He had slept through the early evening until dawn. *Why would a little girl have my harmonica? And what's with the violent pigs? And that serpent?* He wasn't sure if there was any meaning behind the nightmare, but he did know he had to find Flint.

# 14

Outside in the foyer, hospital visitors were sucking down cigarettes, one after the other, and chatting on cell phones. Brad thought about bumming one to clear his head before he went inside. Nothing calmed the old nerves like a coffin nail. He walked by the clouds of nicotine as the visitors puffed away. They had large stickers with their names on them, a room number in the corner, stuck to their chests. His thoughts of falling off the nicotine wagon were interrupted by a golden retriever named Hank.

Hank approached Brad and laid low by his feet. His big dark eyes looked up at Brad, over to the smokers, then back to Brad, as if to say *You better not!* Brad reached down and scratched behind Hank's cozy ears. Hank showed his appreciation by licking Brad's arm.

"C'mon Hank! We got to go!"

Brad didn't realize that old Hank was on a leash. On the other end was a lady in her late fifties. She reminded Brad of her high school English teacher. She wore thick brown frames that magnified matching eyes. She was respectfully dressed and her auburn hair was blowing in her face.

"He does this to me every Thursday," she said. "He hates leaving the hospital." She tugged on the leash but Hank didn't budge. He just laid there and kept his eyes on Brad.

"He's a good boy, aren't you Hank?" Brad said. He ran his

hand through the dog's long blonde hair. It felt good and safe, a necessary distraction for someone with a terminal illness.

"That he is. Hank volunteers here at the hospital once a week. He's a therapy dog. He visits the patients, you know, comforts them." She pulled on the leash again, this time with both hands, and successfully brought Hank to his four paws.

"C'mon, ya big lug!" And with that, Hank led the woman to the parking garage as she said "Hope we don't see you here next week!" with a wave.

"Yeah," Brad said. "Me too."

Diana was still knocked out from meds when Brad entered her room. Her casted leg was elevated by a harness. Her arms bruised yellow and purple from the accident.

*Shame on me. It wasn't another suicide attempt.*

He found a stool and scooted it next to the bed that his wife recovered on. He held her cold, fragile hand. Brad never gave himself the chance to apologize about the fight. Truth is, he always was a little jealous about her success, even if she did have "fuck me" eyes. He shouldn't hold those eyes against her. Hell, those eyes were one of the many reasons why he married her. So deep and mysterious, full of wonder. But every once in a while, that little maggot of jealously would find its way back inside, wiggling its way into his head like a repressed memory. Now, here she was, laying in a hospital bed. Innocent and fractured.

It did occur to Brad to call Madeline's mother to tell Penny what happened. But he waited for Diana to wake up. This type of news should be delivered in person. *I'll call her as soon as I know Diana is okay.*

There was a tap at the door, followed by a "Hello"? It was

Nurse Sally with a clipboard under her arm. "You must be the husband Brad." She extended her hand. "I'm Sally, the nurse. We spoke earlier."

"Yeah I am. How is she?"

"It was a nasty accident. The Jeep went off the road. Her tibia is broken, but it was a clean break. She'll be in a cast for a while, but she'll be safe to go home soon."

Brad placed his hand on Diana's forehead. Her eyelids slowly opened. "Penny," she whispered.

"She's okay, honey," Brad said. "She's with Madeline."

"No, NO!" Diana said. She sat up, blinking her eyes into focus.

"What do you mean, no?"

"We were together...then gone..." Her voice was still groggy from the sedatives.

A single tear fell from Diana's bruised face. The heart monitor picked up, beeping faster and faster. Nurse Sally injected Diana with a clear solution. The monitor went back to a steady pace. *Beep....Beep....Beep*

"Lost control of Jeep...when I came to...she was gone..."

"You were the only one at the scene, ma'am," Nurse Sally said. "You mean your daughter was with you at the time of impact?"

Diana nodded her head slowly.

Nurse Sally gasped. Her eyes big. They met Brad's concerned face. "I'm calling the sheriff, Mr. Carter."

"Thought she...called for help..."

Brad released his wife's hand. He followed the nurse out of the room.

He didn't hear Diana whispering, almost to herself, "I'm sorry..."

# 15

Sheriff Mills arrived to the crash scene later in the day. He ran his stubby fingers through his gray bushy mustache as he reviewed the notes he took from his conversation with Diana:

*Female, 8 years old — 4' 6", 57 pounds*

*Brown hair, hazel eyes, freckled*

*Last seen with mother heading south on State Route 83*

*Mother knocked out after impact*

*Resident for one month — no relationships in town*

He folded his spiral notepad, tucked it back in his khaki chest pocket, and removed his aviator sunglasses, rubbing the bridge of his nose with his finger and thumb.

*Goddam it's a hot one. Too hot to be outside.*

Into his voice recorder, he spoke about his observations:

"Jeep was banged up pretty good. Only thing unusual is the passenger safety belt. It's frayed. Like someone sawed through it to cut missing child free."

He tried to pry open the passenger side door, but it was no use. There was no reasonable way to free the mangled metal. He walked around to the driver's side and clambered into the jeep.

"Straw hat, Exhibit A. Has blue polka dots all over it."

Mills laid the torn end of the seat belt in his open palm. He studied the tear, trying to figure out what was used to rip it. Removing a handkerchief, he wiped hot sweat from his face.

"No blood from the girl. Only blood from what I assume

to be the mother's—down by the brake pedal. There's a little splatter on the steering wheel."

Mills got out and took a long look down State Route 83. He once again motioned his fingers through his mustache and removed his talkie.

> Deputy Wolfe. It's Mills.

> Come in sheriff.

> I don't have the slightest clue where that little girl could've gone. Unless she took a run through the brush, which I doubt she could, seeing's how banged up her mother is. This is going to end up being a missing child's case.

> Yeah?

> Looks like it. I'll meet you back at the station. Did Brenda bring that pie over like she said?

> Yup. I'm looking right at.

Mills placed his hand on his holster and looked down the opposite side of the empty road. The air was hot and the cicadas were singing. The sun, relentless.

> Okay then. Over.

> Over and out, sheriff.

# 16

Daryl thought he could get Flint's home address from the high school's main office. He knew the school would be open because the teachers still had to grade final exams and prepare year-end report cards. Daryl's plan was to wait for the secretary to leave her desk at lunchtime. Then he would sneak in and look up the address in the school directory.

He parked his pick-up on the side of the school, next to the weight room. The double doors were open and he could hear the sounds of iron rise and fall over loud heavy-metal music. Someone shouted, "Seven-eight-nine…c'mon man you got it…ten!"

Daryl slipped into the main entrance and glanced through the Plexiglas office windows. It was empty. Then the down the hallway. Coast was clear.

An email to the faculty was left open on the monitor when Daryl approached it. He minimized it with a click of the mouse and searched the labeled folders on the desktop: Attendance, Honor Roll, Summer School Roster (poor saps), and finally…Directory.

*Bingo.*

He double-clicked the folder to find a series of sub-folders, labeled by each grade. Flint Vangundy was a Junior. He clicked the appropriate folder which opened a file to all the names and emergency contact information of every Junior at Edlund High. He quickly scrolled down to row 'V'.

There he was, Flint Vangundy, the prick who stole his harmonica. Daryl scribbled his phone number and address on a sticky note. He closed the file and found the folder marked 'Seniors'. He scrolled down until he found Sid's last name, Farley, son of Brisco and Jackie. He wrote down his address below Flint's information. A little revenge was in order.

A loud whistling echoed down the hallway. Daryl looked to his right and saw a janitor mopping the floor. He wore headphones and was pushing his mop right in front of the office.

Daryl stuffed the sticky note into his pocket and crawled under the desk. He crouched there for a while, thinking of an alibi.

*I was eager to find out if I passed Social Studies so I decided to come in to see if my exam was graded.*

Too lame. The whistling grew louder as the janitor grew closer. Daryl could hear the mop make its sloppy way toward the office.

*As long as they don't search you, you'll be fine. You already have what you came for. Just play dumb.*

Just before the janitor entered the office, someone yelled "Gordon!" It sounded like Mr. Turnberry, the principal. Turnberry was no push-over. He had a bald, shiny head and intimidating posture. He was a linebacker for Edlund State and would've gone pro had he not blown his knee out his senior year.

"Yes sir!" said Gordon, removing the headphones.

"I need you in the weight room," Turnberry said. "Someone spilled a gallon of that protein shit all over the floor. It's everywhere!"

Daryl always found it peculiar whenever he heard a member of the teaching staff swear. It was one of those things that you don't think they ever do. Things must be kept pretty loose around the school grounds once classes are over, Daryl thought. Wouldn't be surprised if they smoked and drank while they roamed the halls.

Daryl peeked above the secretary's desk to see Gordon lug his mop bucket down the hall.

"Hurry up," Turnberry said, "before someone breaks their goddam neck!"

With Gordon and Turnberry out of sight, Daryl snuck around the desk, outside the school, and back to his pick-up.

———————

Daryl recognized Flint's address. It was on County Road 11, the same road he took to work. He followed the winding road through fields of tall corn. He was almost to Flint's place when he saw four guys in cut-off tee shirts drinking beer under a shady oak tree. Daryl saw Sid first. Flint had to be with him. He always was. Sure enough, as he got a little closer, Daryl saw Flint sitting on the tailgate of a truck smoking a cigarette.

Flint's upper lip curled to a spiteful grin when he noticed Daryl approaching them. He greeted him with a loud belch. "Look boys, if it ain't old Daryl the Animal, fuckin' sheep 'til the cows come home!" He blew a puff of smoke in Daryl's face as he held up the harmonica.

"You looking for this?"

Flint waved the harmonica in Daryl's face, like a cruel owner would wiggle a steak in front of a hungry dog. Daryl reached for it. Flint tossed it to Sid, who was now standing behind Daryl. Daryl went for Sid, who passed it back to Flint.

"Monkey in the middle," said one of the guys.

"More like sheep-fucker in the middle," said Flint.

"Yeah, I like this game," added Sid. "What do you think of it, Daryl the Animal?"

Daryl stood his ground, unwavering. He didn't care if he was outnumbered. This went beyond stealing his personal property. Much more was on the table. The band and, more importantly, Samantha coming to see him perform were the two biggest things Daryl had going for him. And Daryl NEVER had anything going for him.

"Just hand it over, Flint." Daryl said.

Flint gave him that asshole snicker Daryl had grown accustomed to over the years.

"What you going to do about it?" Flint said. "In fact, I'm kinda tired of asking that…"

Daryl grabbed Flint by his skinny throat, swung his hip forward, and delivered a right hook into his nose. Blood splattered between Flint's eyes, now watered.

Holding his face, Flint screamed, "Motherfucker sucker punched me. Did you guys see that?"

Daryl felt a hard thud against the back of his knee, bringing him down to all fours.

*Now I'm in trouble.*

The other two guys jumped from the tailgate and assaulted Daryl with a series of kicks to his ribcage. Daryl's face hit the dirt hard. His heart raced. His stomach turned.

Sid pushed them backward. "That's enough. Ain't even a fair fight. This here's between Daryl and Flint."

Sid scooped Daryl by his underarms and held him up. He locked his hands behind Daryl's head, putting him in a full-nelson. Daryl fell to his knees. Flint hocked up a bloody lunger and spat it on Daryl. Flint's mucous dangled from Daryl's left ear lobe like an opal earring. Flint cracked his knuckles and threw a bony right into Daryl's jaw, followed by a left jab to his right eye, blurring Daryl's vision.

"Fuck, my nose hurts!" Flint said, rubbing his fist. "Pull him back up Sid. I'm not done with this little bitch yet."

"He's had enough," Sid said. "Look at him."

Daryl was sprawled out on the dirt. His eye was swollen and his lip was fat. Flint raised his leg to stomp on Daryl's throbbing head. Sid grabbed him by the shoulders.

"I said he had enough. Word gets to coach about this and I won't get my diploma."

"Who cares? School's out."

"I'm not out of the woods until that diploma is in my hands," Sid said. "Got it?"

"Yeah," Flint said. "I guess you're right."

He stood over Daryl. His long shadow stretched across the dirt road. "You're lucky I'm feeling generous today." He tossed the harmonica next to Daryl. It tumbled in the dirt. The once beautiful harp now lay covered in a brown tint of dust like an unwanted nickel. "That piece of shit don't work anyway."

They climbed into the truck and threw their empty beer cans at Daryl as he slowly crouched over. "Tell your Momma I said hi!" Flint said as they drove away.

Daryl hoisted himself up using the front bumper of his pick-up. He spat a loogie of his own. A wad of snot hit the dirt and wiggled, a bloody jellyfish. He carefully removed his flannel, turned it inside out, and wiped his ear.

A bright reflection in the road caught his eye. He winced in pain as he bent over to pick up his harmonica. He dusted if off and placed it to his mouth, blowing with minimal effort. A note rang through the cornfield and echoed down the road. He felt a warm sensation run through his body. They were finally back together.

Daryl didn't have to struggle much to lock the seatbelt. He caught his image in the rearview mirror. The swelling in his eye and lip was already beginning to go down. Even his ribs were feeling better.

He placed his harmonica in the console and rubbed it like a magic lamp.

"C'mon friend. We have a show to play."

# 17

When you're scared and you're alone, you begin to repent for all the bad things you've done and start making promises to God. For Penny, it was "I'll never talk back to my parents ever again. I won't make fun of anybody. I'll eat my vegetables. I'll be the good girl that I know I can be."

She hobbled over to a bucket in the corner of the room. It was marked WASTE. She wiped the rim of it clean from cob webs, hovered, and relieved herself.

*Thank God I only have to go number one.*

She scanned the room. A school desk was turned over on its side in the corner. Next to it were cardboard boxes, labeled with different subjects: Math, Science, and Biology.

After cleaning herself off, Penny eased herself to the stack of boxes, dragging the heavy chain behind her. She stood on her tip-toes and removed a flap on the box marked BIOLOGY. She took a peek. It was hard to tell what exactly was inside, but the obvious shapes gave the contents away. Tiny skulls piled on top of various bones.

*Other little girls.*

The weight of the chain pulled Penny backwards, causing her to fall. She took the box of bones with her. They sounded like dominos clicking together as the box fell next to her feet. A few of those skulls rolled out onto her chest. She squealed, then quickly covered her mouth and crawled back toward the feed bags.

Heavy footsteps began stomping on the floor above her. She heard muffled whispers through the air vents. The basement door swung open for a moment, then slammed shut. Penny bit her bottom lip and hoped nobody would come down the steps. Nobody did. Yet.

She let her head rest between her knees and prayed this was a nightmare. That this was one of those times she fell asleep after sneaking into her father's office to look at the books he had. She couldn't understand all of the vocabulary, but found the black and white images of mug shots and murder scenes oddly fascinating. The tools used to treat the criminally insane made her feel funny. But she was drawn to them somehow. Maybe it was because she knew she wasn't supposed to be snooping around, maybe it was because they were in black and white, making them more terrifying. But the pain she felt made her realize this was no nightmare. This was definitely real.

There was no teddy bear to comfort her. No Mommy and Daddy to check her closet for boogiemen. There was no dreamcatcher. It was only her, in this concrete prison, and whatever monsters lurked upstairs.

# 18

Two old timers were sitting at the bar when Daryl walked into the Elkhorn. They shielded their faces as the late afternoon light flooded through the open door. They eyed Daryl, pouring their bottled beer into pint glasses, as he approached the bar.

"You must be the hot shot Jud and Scooter been talking about," the bartender said, blowing a pink bubble from her wrinkled lips. Her face was just as wrinkled and served as evidence that she had had her share of good times. The sleeves and collar were torn from her tee shirt, faded black. RATFINK was printed across the chest in red, matching her lipstick. It was only fitting that she had on tight, acid-wash jeans.

"What'll it be, handsome?"

"Ginger Ale please, ma'am."

"If you want anything from me, you'll stop the ma'am talk right now. Save that for your mother."

"Um, sorry," Daryl said. His cheeks burned with embarrassment. The bartender bent over to get Daryl his ginger ale. The old timer's eyes locked onto her bottom as she did. A crude smile on their face. It was all a little out of place for Daryl. He wasn't used to not calling a woman by "ma'am", let alone witnessing two men old enough to be his Grandpa getting enjoyment out of one bending over.

Daryl laid a five spot on the bar and joined the band as they set up their instruments. They looked the part. Blue jeans, solid color shirts…tattoos. They were also much older than Daryl, by twenty years easy.

"Whammer Jammer!" Scooter said, tuning his bass guitar. "C'mon up here and meet the guys." He wrapped his arm around Daryl. "You already know Jud." Jud gave him a wink. "That big burly fella behind the drum kit is Luke." Luke stood up and extended his hand. Tufts of hair sprouted from his shirt collar. "And that one in the corner is Elijah, on organ." Elijah raised his fist, smoking a clove wrap. It reminded Daryl of the way his Grandma smelled, flowery and sweet.

"We ready?" he asked.

"Whoa!" Jud said. "What happened to your face? You get in a tussle on the playground?"

Daryl rubbed the dark crescent shape under his eye.

"You should see the other guy!" Daryl said, making the men chuckle.

"Forget the shiner. You going to be able to play with that lip?"

"Only one way to find out," Scooter said. "Plug in, boys!"

They jammed. The harmonica slid back and forth through Daryl's mouth with ease. That familiar tingling sensation, like he stuck his tongue on a flashlight battery, began. But, unlike his first encounter here, he was in control.

The bartender joined the old-timers as they bobbed their heads to Luke's backbeat. One of them stuck his fingers in his mouth and whistled. Yup. They were into it. The band played on for about fifteen minutes until Jud snapped a guitar string.

"Son of a bitch," Jud said, removing the broken string. "Don't be concerned fellow bandmates. I have more." He turned to Luke, Elijah, and Scooter. They huddled and whispered to each other. Scooter turned his head, his arms still wrapped around the other men, then returned to the huddle. Daryl tapped the harmonica inside of his open hand, anxious.

"We've come to a decision," Scooter said. "You can play with us tonight under one condition."

"What condition is that?"

"That your promise not to blow us off the fucking stage!"

Daryl exhaled. Luke, Elijah, and Jud patted him on the back.

"Show starts at seven-thirty," Scooter said. "Don't be late."

# 19

"I can't even begin to tell you how happy I am to have the whole house to myself," Kelly said. Her brown hair was in a ponytail, her bikini a two-piece, and her drink of choice, a wine cooler. She was the same age as Samantha. They went to different universities after high school and were determined to stay BFF's despite studying miles away from each other.

"Do you have anything stronger?" Samantha said.

"There's bourbon in my Dad's liquor stash. He keeps it in his office. Second door down the hall."

Summer break. Samantha's favorite time of year. All she had to work on was her tan, good old register seven at Jimbo's Market, and a comfortable buzz. She found the bourbon in a crystal decanter on top of a large oak desk. Kelly's dad was a defense attorney whose commercials ran late at night on television. He was somewhat of a local celebrity. People in town considered him a gag because of his over-the-top advertisements. Mainly the one where he's walking toward the camera down a seemingly endless hallway, pointing his finger—"Justice is a right. And if you've been wronged, call the law offices of Devin Franklin. We play hard ball."—then the scene would cut to an image of Devin in a baseball uniform hitting a baseball. *Pop!* Nobody ever knew if the ball went over the outfield wall. He just swung the bat and the ball went flying through the air. End scene. The commercial must've worked because Samantha was standing in his half a million dollar home, and was about to drink his expensive bourbon. She poured herself a drink, three fingers high, into a glass. She let the first sip linger in her mouth before she swallowed, then she winced, and joined Kelly on the patio.

Kelly was stretched out on a beach towel wearing sunglass that covered half her face. "What's the plan, Stan?"

"So glad you asked, Jax. I happen to know of someone playing in a band tonight at The Elk." She whirled her finger around in the brown liquid, then sucked it from her finger tips.

Kelly turned her head, faced her, and slid her sunglasses down her nose. "You can't be serious. The Elk? Are you trying to hook up with a diseased biker or something?" She tuck her tongue out and turned her thumb upside down.

"No slut, I'm not. There's this guy at work who's in a band that's playing there tonight, that's all. Well, probably. He has to audition. But the band is playing regardless."

Kelly joined Samantha at the patio table. "Is that so?" She reached into her bikini top and provided a joint for them to smoke. "Then let's smoke this now, decide later."

"You've been holding out on me all afternoon? You bitch!"

Kelly stuck the joint in her mouth and put her feet on Samantha's lap. "Half now, half later. This is some strong shit." She lit the joint. "Now rub my feet, minion."

Samantha didn't rub Kelly's feet but she did smoke the joint. She let the hot smoke fill her lungs, holding it in for a moment before she exhaled as she reclined back in the patio chair. She sank, full immersion. Term papers, boys with popped collars, five dollars left over in her bank account each week — she let it all drift into the hot July air. Then, thoughts of her childhood: her first period, babysitting, her first kiss. Her birthday party when Kelly farted just before blowing out sixteen candles on a sheet of cake. Then prom. She expanded all of these images into billboard size and watched as she sent a black wrecking ball through them. They shattered to pieces like crystalized graffiti. Now, it was just Samantha, floating among the bright, blue sky in a stellar vortex of relaxation. No regret. No worry.

"This is some good shit," Samantha said.

# 20

If burying your own child is a parent's worst fear, then coping with a missing one has to be a close second. Being questioned as a suspect? Definitely third. But Diana still answered all the sheriff's questions, with the hopes that he would come up with the answers for where her daughter was.

"Like I said, sheriff, I was knocked unconscious. When I came to, she was gone. Next thing I know, I'm in the hospital with my husband. I know she's out there. Somewhere. A parent just knows. Did you search the field? The forest? Did you stop at random homes along the road with the idea that maybe she called for help? I suggest you stop wasting our time and start looking for our daughter."

That's how the interview (interrogation) went between Diana and Mills. And although that last part about her suggesting him to get off his ass and start doing his job made her feel better, one fact still remained: Penny was missing.

---

"I feel so worthless in this cast," she told Brad while he slept in the chair next to her. His head was angled in the way a dog's will angle when it's curious. She fumbled around the bedside and found the awkward hospital TV remote. She clicked through the soap operas, the talk shows, and the court cases that make up daytime programming. Fed up with the lack of entertainment, she reached for her book.

Usually she would have her tablet. But since Brad came straight from the library (and she wasn't expecting to be shacked up in a hospital bed for two days), she was stuck with a novel from the gift shop. In this case, it was a common bestseller about Lance Romance, a former male dancer turned private eye. He was hired by Chloe Chastain to solve the mystery of her murdered husband. Chloe was beautiful in all the right places and played the perfect damsel to Lance. Diana knew where the story was going. Lance would solve the murder—it was Chloe all along—and fall in love with her as he did. Regardless of the plot, the writing wasn't bad and it did pass the time until the doctor released her from the hospital.

# 21

Dusk had arrived by the time Samantha parked her Beetle next to Daryl's pick-up. The Elk's gravel parking lot was full of motorcycles and various trucks. Some with flames on the side, others with testicular steel below the bed. *Does anybody drive a four-sedan in this town anymore?* Kelly pointed to a row of eighteen-wheelers. A dumpster sat next to them.

"That's where they throw the lot lizards when they're done with em," she said, placing drops of solution into her blood shot eyes. A man who appeared to be on a steady diet of cheeseburgers and deep-fried anything stepped over a trailer hitch from behind the dumpster. Patches of urine darkened the denim below his pot belly from where he didn't shake properly. A small cigar bobbed in his mouth when he spoke.

"How would you know, doll?" he said. "You two looking for some action?"

His deep, bellowing laugh turned into an uncontrollable cough. He leaned against the side of the tavern and hacked up something fierce before vomiting on the ground.

"Fucking gross!" Samantha said.

"Creep-o!" Kelly said, showing the guy her middle finger as he spewed. "Are you sure this is a good idea girl? We aren't even in the bar yet and already we're being hit on by nasties."

"I dunno, Kell." Samantha said, tightening her shirt against her chest. "I think he liked us."

Kelly rolled her eyes. "Slut."

All the components that make up a road side bar were present inside: bikers, barflies, boozers, smokers, snorters, and all around good timing party people. The air was hot and stunk of sweat and stale beer. The tiled floor was sticky. Every so often, the smack of a cue ball could be heard over loud debates about politics, sports, or whether or not The Stones were better than Zeppelin. Somewhere in the corner, a biker had his girlfriend for the evening on top of his shoulders as she lobbed darts toward a bullseye. It was another Friday night at The Elkhorn Tavern.

The girls made their way through the commotion and found a small table at the corner of the stage.

"This place is insane!" Kelly said.

"I know!" Samantha looked over her shoulder and took a sip from her flask. She tried to sneak it under the table to Kelly, but she refused it.

"I'm driving your car tonight, alkie. Remember?"

"Suit yourself, doll!" Samantha replied and took one more swig of Mr. Franklin's bourbon before putting it back in her purse.

Outside, behind the tavern, the band prepared for the gig with what Daryl referred to as "funny smoke". They passed a joint between each other while Daryl paced around them.

"We go on in five," Scooter said. "You want to hit this?"

Daryl held up a dismissing hand and continued to pace.

"Whoa dude! Come here. Let me see your face," Jud said. He put his forefingers on Daryl's chin and titled his face against the humming light that lit the exit door.

"Your shiners gone! Hey guys, come take a look at this."

Luke, Elijah, and Scooter joined Jud and they marveled at Daryl's recovery.

"Damn, son," Luke said. "You got some kind of mojo in that harp of yours or something?"

"Either that or this dope got us good," added Elijah, laughing.

Daryl lifted his head away and took a step back. "I don't know. I practiced a little in my truck before I came back here. I guess I didn't notice."

"That's the damndest shit if I've ever seen it," said Scooter. "Let's go."

The tavern lights dimmed around the bar and above the stage. Each member of the band was greeted with fluttering applause as they settled into position. Daryl was last. Just like his hero Johnny Cash, he was dressed in all black: cowboy cut jeans and leather boots that accentuated his shirt—western-style with silver collar tips that were engraved with the American flag on each end. It was tucked behind his belt that was fastened by a silver buckle. Two revolvers crossed each other at the barrel. He left his Stetson at home. Daryl didn't want to overdress. After all, this wasn't The Grand Ole Opry.

Samantha smiled at Kelly as the room grew still. "Tell me that isn't him," Kelly said, pointing at Daryl. Samantha furrowed her brow and kicked Kelly's shin.

Daryl wiped his face with his camouflaged handkerchief, then tucked it away with a nervous hand. Over several coughs, a deep, baritone voice shouted "C'mon and bring it boys!" This was followed with more whistling and applause.

Jud leaned into Daryl. "Relax, man. Give them what they want."

Daryl removed the microphone from his stand and joined it to his harmonica, now pulsing as he placed it to his mouth. In the key of B, Daryl let loose twenty chords of rockabilly. Luke began hitting his kick drum as the rest of the band slowly joined in. Those sharp whistles from the crowd returned, echoing through the tavern as they covered 'Johnny 99' by Springsteen.

Then the lights illuminated the stage. Although they had a lot of miles, they were extremely bright, blinding Daryl just after he spotted Samantha to his right. The sight of her helped him ease into rhythm. Maybe he should've worn his Stetson, Grand Ole Opry or not. At least he would've been safe from those hot lamps.

He felt alone as he worked through various chords. It was as if a single spotlight was on him. The sounds from the other instruments were drowning out. His breath was getting heavy. Something was controlling his lungs.

Jud finished the last lyric as the harmonica sped through E, B, and F Sharp progressions. The band could no longer keep pace. All Luke could do was keep a simple backing beat as Daryl's harmonica became a part of him and took over. No longer a slim, metal instrument, but a fleshy coated limb of his anatomy. An aura of warm light permeated around his hands as he turned his back to the crowd and faced Luke.

Luke's jaw fell open. His wide eyes blinked several times, meeting the other musicians' to see if they were seeing what he was seeing. Luke stood up, ending the constant thud from his drum kit. Daryl kept wailing away.

The riffs accelerated and the chords bended, mesmerizing the audience who were all mostly standing by now. Samantha and Kelly covered their mouths with astonishment. And by the time Daryl's last note of the evening sustained with suspense, hanging in the balance between music and magic, everybody was on their feet.

The harmonica fell from Daryl's mouth and onto the stage. He picked it up, held it for a moment, and caressed it. Then he looked up at the still audience. He didn't know why, but the first person he noticed was the bartender, who had a cigarette hanging from her bottom lip. She ignored the smoke that was drifting into her eyes. A few people clapped their hands. That same baritone voice shouted "Hell yeah! Play it again!" and those sharp whistles returned, urging the band to continue over a thunderous applause.

The harmonica had sucked the energy out of Daryl. He was exhausted and knew he couldn't play anymore. His head hurt. His chest, heavy. Jud and Scooter raised Daryl's arms like he just won the heavyweight title. First round knockout. The stage lights dimmed, the floor lights went up, and Daryl winked at a smiling Samantha.

"We're going to take a break," Jud said, addressing the crowd through his microphone. "Go get a beer. We'll be right back."

---

Outside, the band regrouped and tried to come to terms with Daryl's mystic ability.

"You guys see that?" Luke said. "Maybe it was the dope, man, I don't know, but it was like he was glowing up there!"

"Or maybe he went to the crossroads and sold his soul for rock n' roll," Elijah said, chugging down half a beer.

"I don't care what it was," Scooter added. "It was fucking awesome."

Daryl raised his head. "I don't think I can play anymore tonight."

"What do you mean you don't think you can play anymore?" Scooter said. "You can't just get up there and jerk the crowd off without giving them more! We're really cooking, man!"

"I think I'm going to ..." Daryl bent over and vomited all over his leather boots.

"Fucking amateur," Scooter mumbled.

Elijah finished his beer, crushed it with his shoe, and kicked it to the side. Daryl's band mates stared at him in disappointment.

"You heard the boy," Elijah said. "He's done. We got to get back in there."

"You'll be back next Friday night?" Jud asked. "Minus the jitters?"

Daryl gave him an affirmative nod, although he wasn't quite sure if he was cut out for it.

"Good," Jud said, putting an arm around him. "Go home. Get better. And make sure you bring those two girlies back with you."

Daryl tilted his head, surprised by the comment, and wiped his mouth with his shirt sleeve.

"Yeah," Jud continued. "I saw them eyeballing you up there. They're too young to be in a place like this, but they sure are cute."

"They sure are. See if they got any older sisters, Daryl," Scooter said as Daryl walked back to his pick-up.

"Prodigy or not, there's something not right with that kid and his harmonica, Jud," Luke said. "And I don't like it. Gives me the willies. Just don't feel right. I swear that harmonica became a part of him. Like an extra limb or something."

Scooter intervened. "Well, he can play and that's what matters. You coming, Jud?"

Jud waved them on as he watched Daryl climb into his pick-up and drive away. Samantha and Kelly weren't far behind him.

"A yellow Beetle," Jud whispered.

"What was that?" Scooter said. "C'mon man, we got to get back in there."

"Yeah man, I'm coming."

# 22

Penny awoke to the sound of a crowing rooster. The morning light was dampened by dirt from a rectangle-shaped window, located at the far-east wall of the basement. She saw tall blades of grass swaying in the breeze and wondered what it would be like to roll in them.

She stared up at the window for some time, thinking about her friends back in the city. They were probably watching cartoons and eating sugary cereal in their pajamas. Her attention switched to the desk in the corner by the stairwell. It was on its side the last time she remembered. The bones were gone and the boxes were now neatly stacked on top of each other. The box marked BIOLOGY was now on the bottom of the stack.

The basement door opened.

A swinging bulb in the center of the basement buzzed to life. It flickered for a moment, emitting a faint, orange hue, then radiated bright, revealing the rusted metal desk and a splintered wooden chair. Large flakes of old paint peeled from its surface and a name, Schott, was crudely carved into its leg.

Footsteps echoed down the stairs. One by one, they became louder, more prominent. Someone marching with a purpose. Penny scurried against the wall with the chain coiled at her feet and rested herself behind a burlap sack, her only protection. She peeked around its side, knowing, but still hoping, that whoever was coming down the stairs wouldn't find her.

A pale foot appeared first. It was attached to a skinny leg, followed by another. Each leg was covered with scratches and open sores. Some were bandaged, others were not. Purple veins stretched vertically behind opaque flesh, an anatomical highway road map.

"It's breakfast time!" said a cheery voice.

Penny clenched the bag tighter against her skin. Its twined surface made her skin itch.

"Will you come out from there, little one?" asked the pleasant, female voice. "I'm not going to hurt you."

Penny heard something being sat on top of the desk. She curled herself together, head down between her legs, wishing for this person to go away.

"Okay. Suit yourself. You'll need your nourishment. Tomorrow we begin our studies!"

Penny waited until she heard the basement door close before she came out of her bunker. A silver platter was on top of the desk. On top of the platter, a glass bottle of milk and a toaster pastry. She was reluctant to consume it, remembering you weren't supposed to accept something from a stranger, but this was a different circumstance. It wasn't like someone was trying to lure her into a van with tinted windows. Besides, she was starved. The milk shake she had two days ago was long digested.

Her mouth watered with saliva as she ripped the foil package open. Icing flaked onto her hands as she shoved chunks of the pastry into her mouth. Its strawberry sweetness made her stomach burn. Then she smelled the milk, as she always did with something she was unsure about. It wasn't sour so she took a big gulp, letting the white liquid run down her chin. The milk coated her stomach, like the pink stuff in the commercial.

The rush of sugar gave her a sudden burst of energy. She yanked at the chain around her waist, trying to make it give. Her hands became dirty with orange rust. Sweat emerged on her brow. It was no use. The chain was too strong, too heavy for her to break it.

Defeated, she sat down on the cold basement floor and wondered if she could ever escape. Her Mom and Dad had to be looking for her. Then it hit her. *The accident. What if Daddy was at Mommy's funeral right now? What if they forgot about me? NO! Never. What if they had Mommy locked away upstairs? And what did that woman mean about studies?* She hoped somebody would find her before her questions could be answered.

# 23

Diana and Brad's first few hours at home were spent in a haze. They couldn't settle in knowing Penny was out there, probably alone. They had put their trust in Sheriff Mills to find her. Based on their meeting with him, however, Diana suspected he was just as clueless of Penny's whereabouts as she was. They decided to take action.

Diana began shuffling through photographs. It was hard to find one where Penny wasn't wearing a faux smile, playing to the photographer at hand. Despite her boisterous personality, she was camera shy. Then she came across her favorite picture of her daughter, taken at the beach last summer.

It was a rare moment where Penny was caught off guard. Brad had let her bury him in the sand. A small beach crab had crawled up his sand-covered stomach, investigating the unfamiliar mound. Then it quickly crawled to his face, snapping its ghostly white claws.

"It's gonna get you, Daddy!" Penny had said, giggling. Brad blew at the crab, trying to shoo it away. It reminded Penny of the story about the three little pigs. She covered her eyes with her hands and peeked at her Dad between her fingers. Just before the crab reached Brad's chin, it scurried away toward the shore.

That's when Diana took the picture of her daughter, Penelope Ann Carter, in the photograph that would become how the small town of Edlund would come to know her little princess. With a purple beach towel wrapped around her tiny frame. With her plastic orange framed sunglasses held between two knotted pigtails. With a face so happy and jubilant, you would've thought it was choreographed. Almost like it was meant to be.

After hours of sobbing and "I can't believe we even have to do this conversation," Brad went to an office supply store in town and printed off copies of the photo. He stapled them everywhere: the post office, the playground, the gas station. Even the mayor held a press conference once word got around. He pleaded to anyone with information to contact local authorities. Local authorities being Sheriff Mills.

Brad's final stop was Jimbo's Market. He placed advertisements for babysitting and lawn care on top of each other to make room for his daughter's photo. "Have You Seen Me?" it asked at the top, below her angelic face. Yes. This was more important than getting a freebie on your first lawn cutting. He placed push pins into each corner of the glossy image.

On his way out, Brad remembered Diana wanted wine. He decided not to go back inside. He knew how people were in a small town, with their gossip and exaggerated opinions. He could hear them now "I'll tell you, that little girl probably ran away." "Her Dad was in Jimbo's buying alcohol for a party just days after she went missing." "I heard he was abusive and that's why they moved here."

He didn't need any of that talk right now. He passed a liquor store on his way in, just before the scene of the accident. It was going to take something much stronger than wine to settle him down.

He was the only customer that afternoon in the liquor store, appropriately named 'Hope's Wine and Spirits.' The man behind the counter looked up from his hunting magazine.

"Help you find anything?"

"No thanks," Brad said. He grabbed a hand basket and headed for the whiskey aisle. After some debating, he opted for a fifth of whisky in a plastic bottle and a six-pack of cold beer in tall cans. Diana wanted something sweet, so two magnum bottles of 'Happy Girl Vino' it would be.

"Will that be all?" asked the clerk, raising his white, bushy eyebrows.

"Pack of smokes, too. In the red box, please." Brad placed a cheap lighter on the counter, the kind that emitted an uneven flame. He gave up smoking when Penny was born, so investing in a good lighter seemed silly. He had no intention on picking up the habit again.

Brad headed south on State Route 83 with the booze stored in a brown paper bag next to him on the passenger seat. The radio was off. Now was not the time to listen to the same two hundred songs in rotation. He needed to think.

He arrived at the scene of the accident. It was obvious where it occurred because huge ruts were still present in the embankment where the jeep crashed. He took a swig of whiskey, opened a beer, and carefully smacked the cigarette pack against his palm. He removed the foil seal and held the filters against his nose. The sweet aroma reminded him of the sleepless nights he spent cramming for exams in college.

Brad sat in his car for a moment, allowing the warm buzz of alcohol filter through his body while he smoked. He took another drink from the bottle when a rush of nausea hit him. He opened the car door and buckled over. Long strands of saliva stretched from his mouth while he gagged. Nothing came up.

*Buying these cigarettes was a bad idea.*

Beer in hand, he walked around to the field, inspecting bloody glass and metal. Prisms of light caught his eye as he searched through the overgrowth, hoping to find something. That same something he was looking for was also telling him he was wasting his time. He was just looking for an excuse to be alone for a moment. He knew from research for his self-published crime novels that the window to find a missing child grew smaller after the first seventy-two hours. It had already been close to sixty since the accident. The window was closing.

# 24

Diana looked down at her crutches with disgust. She told Brad earlier that she needed to exercise her good leg in order to stay healthy. She was determined to not be confined by a wheelchair. She also had told him to trash all the junk food in the house. The pantry was now stocked with her requests: rice cakes, pumpkin seeds, and raisins.

*Rabbit food.*

Diana settled for a jar of almond butter to curb her hunger. She swirled the creamy texture around with a spoon before shoving it into her mouth and chasing it down with iced tea.

Brad also made her a make-shift studio in the dinette area so she wouldn't have to climb the stairs to her office. All of her paints, brushes, and pencils were assorted along a small bench that used to be in the living room. Her office chair was brought in so she could easily roll back and forth between the canvas and supply station.

It was difficult getting back to work. The deadline for her project was approaching. She was assigned to create a movie poster for a film about a young medium. The medium befriends an elderly man and helps him grieve by communicating with his deceased wife. A typical supernatural feel-good movie with an A-List cast. The film wasn't of her interest, but it paid the bills.

She stared at the blank canvas, waiting for inspiration to come. It didn't. She decided to release her emotions and just paint what she felt — remorse. This translated to a portrait of a young woman with her hands deep in her denim pockets. The woman stared into the distance, a blank expression, her shoulders hunched as she kicked at loose gravel across a vacant lot. The painting was of her.

Diana looked at the sketch for a moment, then took a red tipped brush to the canvas, corner to corner, and slapped it off the easel with a frustrated hand.

Journaling had always been a healthy outlet for her. It helped her to gain perspective and to manifest her feelings without regret. Her last entry was six months ago and she was disappointed in herself for getting away from it. But that's what we do sometimes. We stop doing the things that worked best once our situation improves. So she opened her journal, wrote the date at the top of the page, and began writing.

*This will be the first time we won't see fireworks together. I knew this day would come, but I expected it to be much later in life, when you were all grown up and had a family of your own. I know you're still alive, pumpkin. I know you're looking up at the sky, wondering where we are. Wondering why we haven't found you yet.*

*She would've come home by now. She's smart enough to find help. I'd love to shove my crutch so far up the sheriff's ass. And if someone has her, God help them. I'll stomp the rubber ends into their eyes, crack the crutch over their head, and piss down their throat. Really make them suffer.*

*Try and match the pain physically that they've
made us feel emotionally because no amount of
prison time can justify this.*

*Daddy and I will do everything we can to get you
back safe into our arms. We will never give up
until we find you. Promise.*

Diana dropped the pen into the spine of her notebook, closed
her eyes, and meditated. She thought of her mantra, reciting
the word over and over. The word expanded through her
thoughts and rotated like a propeller, spinning through
cosmic space. Then it shrank. She pulled it back, closer so
she could see it. The word, *shama*, glowed in neon color,
shrinking and expanding like an inflating balloon before it
burst. A slideshow of memories moved through her mind.
Diana as a young girl, riding on her tricycle. The time she
was cut from the cheerleading squad. Her wedding. Finally,
the happiest day of her life, Penelope's birth. Diana held this
image of her holding her only child until it
dissipated—floating away into a dark nothing.

# 25

Gregory Mills grew up in Edlund. And like most people who grow up in a small town, he never left. And in all his ten years as sheriff, he had never encountered a missing person's case. A missing house pet? Sure. He had cracked many of those. A lost puppy or cat that went astray from the home-front, making little girls and boys sad, but never an actual person. Of course, over the years, there were missing person cases in the surrounding counties, some of which did involve children, but never did it happen here, not in Edlund, not in *his* county.

So when Penelope Carter became missing from an automobile accident, he wasn't quite sure how to approach it. Honestly, he would've been happy to retire without having to deal with that sort of thing. Most sheriffs would, he supposed. But he was lazy, and trying to find a lost child required a lot of work, he also supposed.

Deputy Wolfe was quite young. Mills thought with time, Wolfe may learn from his naivety, and one day be prepared to take over for him as sheriff once he retired.

Wolfe had all the physical characteristics for a law enforcer. He was thin, athletic, and had the kind of personality that people would often open up to. Unfortunately, he was still green around the collar when it came to handling conflict so it only made sense that he would pass the buck to his superior when Brad decided to visit them.

"Mr. Carter is here," he said through the speaker phone. "He wants to talk to you about his girl. Should I send him in?"

"Give me a moment," Mills responded. He shuffled some papers around his desk to make it look like he was busy with the investigation. Then he opened the drawer from underneath his desk and removed a canteen. People deal with conflict in different ways. Wolfe passed it over to his sheriff. Mills handled it with whiskey. He poured some into his coffee mug. Ironically, it was decorated with the words "The Buck Stops Here". On the other side, "I'm Buck." It wasn't the most professional way to go about business, but it certainly took the edge off when a little girl's parents were depending on you to find her.

Mills took a long sip from the flask before putting it back in the drawer. Out of all twelve buttons on his office phone, the speaker and hold functions were the only two he ever used, or knew how to.

"Okay. Send him in."

Brad entered the office, looking awful. He hadn't slept well the past few nights and the drinking began to take a toll on him. It was as if he had been roaming around an unknown country, unable to understand its foreign language.

"Morning sheriff. I'm Brad Carter, Penny's father. You spoke to my wife at the hospital."

"Yes," Mills replied with a welcoming handshake. "I know who you are and I'm sorry we have to meet like this."

"Diana wanted to come with me, but with her leg and all…we just decided it best she stayed at home."

"That's quite alright, Mr. Carter. Please, have a seat."

Brad got comfortable and looked around the office. The

walls were covered with framed recognition certificates from the mayor and photographs of deep-sea fishing trophies. Brad's eyes caught the attention of one in particular. A marlin suspended by wire, the Pacific Ocean in the background providing an additional highlight. The marlin's bleak eyes were uninspiring between its long, pointed bill. Mills was wearing a Hawaiian shirt, its collar uneven as he wore a smile that had triumph written all over it. He was standing next to a charter guide who wore thick, rubber overalls and a worn baseball cap with a fish hook clasped to the bill. A once thriving predator in the vast ocean was now a trophy for its greatest predator: Man. Brad related the marlin's vulnerable position to his own current one.

"You like to fish?" Mills said.

"Not particularly, no." Brad's eyes shifted back to the sheriff. "The ocean terrifies me."

"Too bad. It's a hell of a rush. I caught that monster five years ago. Wrestled with it for over an hour."

*Maybe you can catch another monster.*

"So what do you do?"

Brad crossed his legs and adjusted himself in the chair.

"I'm a writer."

"Oh yeah? What do you write?"

"Fiction. Crime fiction. Kind of ironic given the circumstance, isn't it?"

After taking a long sip from his coffee mug, Mills finally replied. "Your daughter's circumstance is far from fiction, Mr. Carter."

"Please, enough with the misters. Call me Brad."

"Okay, Brad. My deputy and I are doing everything we can

within our right to find her. We already spoke with everyone in town. There aren't any witnesses as of yet. But we're confident that..."

"And the field. You searched the field where the crash took place, didn't you? I only ask because I saw a farmhouse not too far from the scene."

Mills found it peculiar that Brad had gone over his head to search into matters himself, even if it did turn out to only be a fly-by. He lit a cigar and propped his feet on his desk.

"That farmhouse has been vacant since I can remember. Lord knows what type of critters are roaming around in there, rent-free. Let us do the digging, the dirty work. I know this town better than anybody. I'm one of its oldest residents." Mills placed his smoldering cigar in the crystal ashtray at the corner of his desk and clasped his hands together.

"The best thing for you to do is go home and comfort your wife. After our talk at the hospital earlier, I have the impression that she blames herself for what happened." Leaning forward—"Am I right?"

Brad blinked behind bleak eyes of his own and nodded.

"I know this is hard. The worrying, the waiting, the uncertainty. But we're determined to find her. And we will."

"Do you think she's still alive? Be honest."

Like a coach assuring a player who has lost confidence, Mills replied. "There's no doubt in my mind she is."

With that affirmation, Brad stood up and shook the hand of Sheriff Mills.

"Be strong for your wife," Mills said. "We'll be in touch."

Brad hung his head and smiled at Deputy Wolfe on his way out. It was the kind of smile you would see on a person of mischief, holding a secret of sorts. Before he exited, Brad turned to Mills and Wolfe.

"You know sheriff, only you and your deputy are on the force," he said, bending his fingers in quotations when he said 'force'. "There aren't any other police officers in town. How do you know you're doing everything possible?"

"The reason there are only two of us is *because* we're in a small town," Wolfe said. "There isn't any need for us to have a great big police force. You have to understand that this thing with your daughter, it doesn't ever happen."

"More the reason to ask for help," Brad said.

"We have this under control, Mr. Carter," Wolfe said.

"I can see that now. Thank you, gentlemen." Brad's sarcasm stung Mills' pride a little as he left the station.

---

"Well I must say that did go better than I expected," Mills said, cigar in mouth. "He has this look in his eyes that I've never seen before in a man."

"His daughter *is* missing."

"Yeah I know, but there's something else there. Something I cannot get my head around."

"Did you tell him about the farm?"

"No, but he asked about it." Mills took a seat across from Wolfe. "I told him it was abandoned and he had no business snooping around there."

"Do you think it's him? Do you think he's back?"

"Who? The Pig Man? Christ, Wolfe! Why you have to bring that up?"

Wolfe spread his hands open as he leaned back in his chair. "I'm just saying!"

Exhausted smoke puffed out of Mills' mouth. "No one knows if he even existed in the first place."

"What do you know about him?"

"It was just some story my father used to tell us as kids to keep us off the Schott's farm property."

Wolfe leaned in with anticipation. "And?"

Rolling his eyes, Mills told the story.

"AND...years ago, according to my Pops, a man was torn apart, limb by limb, after seeing the Pig Man. The man was hunting on the Schott Farm property. Sometime later, this must've been early to mid-seventies, a group of teenagers were partying in an open field, way out on the edge of the Schott's land. Their bodies were mutilated, eaten by what appeared to be a sounder of pigs. The way he told it, it was as if the sounder came from nothing and left the same way."

Mills rolled his cigar along the rim of an ashtray, watching flakes of ash dance before they fell.

"This Pig Man, he was teased by the other children for being a poor farmer's boy. He went to school every day in the same overalls, reeking of pig shit. It didn't help that he also had round, plump cheeks and a pudgy nose. One day, Pig Man was cleaning out the sty on the family farm. He fell in. The pigs ate him alive. Legend has it that his ghost roams those farm fields, taking his revenge out on those who dare to trespass on his family's land."

"Those farm fields being the ones that Mr. Carter's family crashed on?"

Mills nodded and looked out the station's front window.

"Yeah. Pig Man had a little brother and sister. They were young when he was supposedly murdered by the animals. But I've never seen them. People make things up you know? Add to the story as it passes down."

"Are we going to check the farm out?"

"I suppose we're going to have to…" Mills took his attention at a boy and his father crossing the street in front of the station, hand-in-hand. "I suppose we will."

# 26

The following morning, Penny was woken up this time by the sound of a steady romp of mattress springs and the moaning of a man and a woman. Although the moans were pleasant, they made her feel uncomfortable, like the time she accidentally saw naked breasts on television. She covered her ears.

Once the racket stopped, she removed her hands to a muffled conversation that came through the basement vent. Then a screen door slammed shut and rattled against a worn door jamb. Then the basement door opened.

Those familiar pale legs came down the stairs, varicose veins and all. White flakes peeled from their surface. The knee caps reminded her of the knobby trunks from the trees she used to climb, ugly and misshaped.

She again shielded herself with the stack of burlap feed bags as the woman made her way to the basement floor. Her hair was gray, highlighted with red streaks. It was matted down to one side. On the other side, a yellow bow, intertwined with damaged roots and split ends. She wore a white dress, patterned with purple flowers, that was tainted yellow from well water. Penny could see the woman's nipples through the fabric. They erected from her sagging breasts, creating a disfigured mound above her stomach, which was damp.

In the woman's hands was a wicker basket. She placed it down on the desk and removed its contents: a heavy book, a

No. 2 pencil, a ruler, and a legal pad. She ran her finger over the pencil tip, testing it for sharpness, and motioned Penny to join her.

"Come on out, little one!" said the woman.

Penny didn't want to upset someone who was capable enough to imprison a child in a basement, so she reluctantly appeared, dragging the heavy chain behind her. The top layer of skin above her ankles was worn to a pink, burning rash. Step by agonizing step, she made her way to the wooden chair. She felt the wood would splinter the underside of her legs, scratching and piercing at her soft skin.

Before she identified herself, the woman interlocked her fingers and rested her hands on her stomach, just over the wet spot. The she opened her mouth, revealing brown, jagged teeth.

*Those teeth could probably chew right through this chain.*

"What's your name, little girl?"

Penny thought about giving the woman a fake name. But if she found out she lied, she might get angry. And if she got angry, she might hurt her.

"Penelope is my name."

"Oh, how cute. Well Penelope, I'm Margaret. You'll refer to me as Ms. Schott and I'll be your instructor. Now that we're acquainted and roll-call has been logged, please open your book to page one."

Penny ran her hand over the heavy book's dust cover. BIOLOGY was printed in gold across the center in bold lettering. Each page had turned yellow from age. She did as instructed and flipped through the pages until she reached the first chapter, Amphibians. The image of a dissected frog stretched across the page, corner to corner. Gall bladder, intestine, stomach, liver—all the inner workings of the frog were labeled. Penny squinted and covered the picture with her hands.

"Our first lesson is anatomy. We will learn each organ and its function. Each week will follow a new lesson. Once you've completed the exams from this book, we'll move on to other subjects, like history, arithmetic, and language. We will do this six days a week." Her enthusiasm was more frightening to Penny than her appearance. "Sundays are reserved for prayer and Bible lessons. You do believe in God, don't you?"

Although the existence of a God that would allow her to be imprisoned by this crazy woman seemed absurd, Penny nodded anyway. Just keep agreeing with her. Don't make her angry.

"Good. That's so great to hear because little girls that don't believe in God go to Hell." She was blunt with her delivery. "Now let's begin."

The flabby skin under Margaret's arms jiggled as she pointed to the different parts of the amphibian with a pencil. "As you can see, from top to bottom, we have the right and left lobe of the gull bladder. Below that are the lungs, stomach, and pancreas." Then she leaned into Penny with rotten breath.

"Can you tell me what the lungs are used for?"

Penny turned her head, disgusted. She didn't understand what Margaret was doing or what she wanted from her. If Penny had to learn this disgusting material, she wanted to do it in the safety of a classroom with a comforting teacher and children her own age. Children she could roll her eyes with.

Margaret put her frail hands on the desk and tapped her

cracked, unpolished fingernails on its surface, creating an uneasy rhythm. Penny noticed that Margaret's dirty cuticles were stained with blood, and before Penny could give her answer, Margaret curled those cuticles away from her and slammed her fist on the desk.

"I asked you a question!"

This brought Penny out of her daydream and into her dark reality. She cupped her hands together and decided to participate. "I can't take notes with my hands tied together like this, Miss Schott." She held her wrists up, bound by fuzzy twine. "Won't you cut them free?"

"I'm the one asking the questions," Margaret said, leaning in closer. Her breath now so unbearable that Penny stopped breathing through her nose so she wouldn't have to smell it. "Now answer me. What are the lungs used for?"

Penny turned her head and sucked in a breath of fresh oxygen through her mouth. "To breathe," she said. "The lungs are used to breathe."

Crossing her arms, Margaret stood up. A thin smile came across her face and she began clapping like a wind-up monkey crashing cymbals together. "Very good. I knew you were a smart one. Not like those other children. I have a word for those children. Stupids. And you're not a Stupid now, are you Penelope?"

Penny shook her head from side to side.

"Now the stomach. It's function?"

"It's where food goes after you swallow it."

"And?"

"And if I eat too many sweets, it makes my tummy hurt. Not

hurt when you have to go number-two real bad, but hurt like it burns."

Margaret's patience grew smaller. "And?"

"And it feels funny when you're up high somewhere, like on an elevator or something."

Margaret lifted the ruler and slapped it on the desk. "NO! The stomach digests food and distributes vitamins and nutrients to the body. And you said you weren't a Stupid."

"I'm not Miss Schott. I'm only eight."

As if speaking to an audience, Margaret outstretched her flabby arms. "She's only eight years old ladies and gentlemen! Give her a round of applause for being so naïve." She grabbed Penny by her chin, squeezed her lower jaw, and said "You're going to have to do better than that if you want your little hands free. Do you understand me?"

Tears were now rolling down Penny's face. No sniffle, no puckering. Just tears.

"Aw, aw, there, there. Do you want something to cry about?" Margaret struck the ruler across Penny's cheek, sending a hot streak of pain through her face. Penny's neck folded to the side.

Margaret approached her from behind and embraced her. Penny smelled a pungent odor leaking from Margaret's underarms. "There, there. It'll be okay. I just need you to listen and pay attention during our studies, okay?"

"I'm scared," Penny said. "I want my Mommy and Daddy. I want to go home."

"You are home sweetie."

# 27

Samantha twirled her key ring around her finger while a cloth apron draped over her shoulder. It was another unbearable day. Daryl passed her in the parking lot, pushing a row of shopping carts, his tongue out like a thirsty lap dog.

"Hey Daryl, nice concert. You can really play!"

"Thanks, yeah... sorry I had to go. Didn't feel so well. I think it was something I ate. You know, food poisoning."

A pink balloon expanded from Samantha's pursed lips as she inflated her bubble gum. It burst. She moved the gum to the back of her mouth, smiled, and continued chewing.

"Sucks, man. You were really smoking up there."

Daryl thanked her again.

"I'm going to a party with my friend Kelly tonight. I'd like it if you went."

"I have to mow my Grampa's grass after my shift. He's getting old. I mean he's already old, but he needs to slow down. His heart's bad."

"Okay. If you change your mind..." She handed him her phone number, scribbled on the back of a grocery receipt. He blushed, but she couldn't tell because his face was already a burnt red from the heat outside.

---

When it came to family, they always came first with Daryl, even if it meant not going to a party with the beautiful

Samantha. But, he also had things on his mind to sort out, like what in the hell was happening to him every time he played the harmonica. And what the deal was with the vision in his dream. He had questions. He needed answers. It was also high time he paid Sid a visit, a one-on-one encounter, to see if he was as brave alone as he was when he was with his buddies.

Once in the lobby of the market, Daryl took a gander at the corkboard where Brad had been earlier. He was looking for a medium, a seer, a tarot card reader, anyone to help him. What he found next to a picture of a rusty tractor someone was selling, was Penny. Her hand over her mouth, hiding a smile. She was happy, safe, and on a sun-soaked beach. Daryl recognized her immediately. She was the girl from his dream.

# 28

Sid sprayed a cloud of pebbled dirt into the air as he put his bicycle down in front of his parent's trailer. He parked it next to the family mutt, Rusty. Rusty was unusual looking, crossed somewhere between a city rat and a feral wolf. Sid's dad found him wandering the road one day on a good afternoon bender. It was the type of bender where the guilt from his life was making him feel vulnerable. He thought having a dog around the place would make things feel like family. But like most things in Sid's life, once his dad sobered up, Rusty only served as something else to kick around.

Sid knew his dad was already drunk. It was evident by the collection of beer cans on the front stoop. Night had fallen and the glow from the television permeated through the trailer's thin curtains. The combination of sweaty feet and sour hops filled Sid's head as the front door sprung shut behind him. The ragged carpet was littered with yellowed cigarette butts. Framed pictures of various wildlife hung from the nicotine stained walls. Deer, bear, mountain lions. These weren't animals that had been hunted by Sid's dad, nor were they actual photographs he took on a nature hike. They were just pictures...probably bought from a flea market.

Two professional wrestlers were beating each other inside of a ring on the tube television that was elevated to eye level by multi-colored plastic crates. Rabbit ears were askew on the top and twisted with aluminum foil, like deranged robotic arms.

As suspected, his dad was passed out on the easy chair, cig burning, beer in hand.

Sid approached the dining room table, his mother's headquarters. Her bottle of prescription painkillers was spilled out next to a coffee can that she used as an ashtray. Bills marked 'PAST DUE' in red were scattered by a newspaper. An eleven-inch black and white television sat on the corner of the table with the same aluminum crown as the one in the living area.

He removed the cellophane from a pack of generic cigarettes he found next to the coffee can and placed two of his mother's pills inside. He rolled the stiff material into a square—carefully, to not wake his dad—and drank the remaining amount of beer that his mother couldn't finish.

*At least she made it to bed.*

Typically, she would've been faced down on the newspaper, conked out from the day's cocktail of pills and booze. Sometimes the ink from the newspaper would transfer to the side of her face. On certain mornings one could read the obituary between her nose and ear.

He tip-toed to the cleanest room in the trailer, his bedroom. The walls were made of cheap wood paneling—a façade for the cabin-feel his parents were trying to create. Posters of muscle cars, women in bikinis, famous rappers, and an enormous marijuana leaf covered the paneling. A variety of football jerseys (many were of players who had moved on to different teams) hung from a metal bar with matching colored fitted hats in his makeshift closet across from his twin mattress. A dark bed sheet served as the closet door, ever since his dad put his fist through the original one during a drunken spell.

Sid pulled a bottle of Mad Dog 20/20 from under his mattress and set it on his nightstand. He removed the cellophane from his pocket and popped a pill in his mouth. He washed it down with the warm, sweet taste of strawberry-grape. He then placed a nudie magazine on his lap and crushed the other pill, still in the cellophane, with his fist.

The pills powdered remains struck his brain instantly, burning his nasal passages. He pinched his nose and held his head back, allowing the drip to seep over his throat. He finished the last line with his other nostril, lit one of his mother's cheap cigarettes, and slipped headphones over his ears. He imagined himself on a grand stage, Madison Square Garden—sold out. A large chain swinging from his neck, a platinum microphone in his hand, and thousands of adoring fans rapping along to his words. He thought about the kind of car he would drive, Bentley, the kind of girl he would date, runway model, and the kind of house he would live in, mansion. A mansion far away from this place.

His dream seemed millions of miles away from his quaint, trailer park bedroom. He just needed his break, man! His opportunity. His moment to show the world his capability to be a rapper. Writing songs in his bedroom wasn't cutting it. He needed access. Someone with a recording studio. Someone who could believe in his talent as much as he did.

His thoughts vanished as he heard a crash in the bathroom across the hall. He paused the stereo, removed the headphones, and pretended to be asleep—leaving just enough room through his eyelids to peek at anyone (his dad) who might be making a visit.

Sid felt the presence of someone in the room. He heard some rustling next to his head, followed by a loud belch, a snicker, and then the sounds of paper being torn. He opened his eyes. His dad was ripping up his notebook, the one with all of his rhymes.

"What the fuck, dad?"

His dad looked like he just saw a ghost. It was as if he was seeing right though his son as he spoke to him.

"What are you doing? STOP IT!"

Sid leaped out of bed and reached for the notebook. His dad raised it above his head while Sid hopped around him, trying to grab it. Those drunken eyes didn't move. Didn't waver. They were lifeless and cold. Finally, Sid's dad tossed the notebook on the bed and grabbed his son by the throat. He squeezed with both hands. Then there was a knock at the door that no one heard.

Outside, Daryl heard commotion from inside the trailer but thought it best not to go in just yet. He peeked through the screen door. The place looked like the inside of a flea market dumpster, full of shit that nobody wanted. Then he heard Sid yell "Stop it" and everything went quiet. Maybe Sid had a girl in his room. What better way to surprise him?

*Maybe he had his pecker out!*

Daryl let the screen door close quietly. He walked down the hallway and listened to the sounds of someone choking, *blowjob?*, before he nudged the door open.

What Daryl saw was nothing he anticipated. A scrawny man with scraggly hair was on top of Sid, choking him, and not just choking him to scare him. The man had his knee on Sid's chest, his thumbs below Sid's Adam's apple, and his elbows were squeezing together for maximum constriction.

Daryl yelled "Stop it, get off him!" The man ignored Daryl, still in a trance of dissipation. Sid's face was red, mouth agape, eyes bulging. There was nothing vengeful about this. Daryl's boot connected with the head of Sid's dad. It rocked back for a moment, his grip still a locked mechanism around his son's throat. Daryl went for the ribs instead. This time, he really put force into it, swinging his leg back and planting his left foot into the dingy carpet. *Crack!* Daryl felt bones break through the tip of his boot. The man moaned and rolled over. Sid rubbed his throat and leaned to the side, catching his breath in between coughs.

After a moment, Sid looked up. "Daryl the fucking animal. What the fuck, dude?" Daryl stood there, making sure Sid's dad wasn't going to try anything else as he lie in the corner, blacked out from either Daryl's punt or the booze. Or both. Probably both.

"This fucking asshole," Sid said, sending a kick of his own into his dad's back, "tore up my fucking notebook." He continued to stomp on him as tears of anger spewed from his eyes. "Fucking loser!" Daryl restrained Sid and pulled him into the hallway. He put Sid against the wall. "He's had enough." Then they walked outside. Sid lit a cigarette.

"You never did answer me," Sid said. "What the fuck? Why are you here?"

"Never mind. I'm just glad I was."

"You come for some payback?"

Daryl turned and walked towards his truck, stepping over

Sid's bike. Rusty was cowering by the porch. The dog knew when the old man was on a war path.

"I could've took him you know," Sid said. "My old man ain't shit!"

# 29

The sky was lit with beautiful stars the night Samantha Swanson went missing. She didn't pay any attention to the truck that followed her to the party or the way it sped passed her, then slowed, as she pulled into the crowded front yard. She did notice a familiar song on the trucks stereo as it passed by, but she couldn't remember from where.

She arrived to the party late, and for good reason. She liked to see how obnoxious and annoying people were when they were drunk. This way, she could pace herself and be in control, and not turn into the next viral video star.

A slow eighties-power ballad played through the stereo as she approached the kitchen. There were boys wearing baseball caps with frayed bills and wanna-be-hippie girls with dirty bare feet playing beer pong, singing along to the arena rock.

Samantha stepped around a couple making-out by a stainless steel refrigerator, littered with greasy fingerprints, and found a handle of whiskey next to a large bowl of shattered potato chips. The kind with the ridges, her favorite. She took a sip from the bottle. Her teeth clamped together. That bite, that sting, was something she would never get used to.

She found a red plastic cup and washed it out with detergent, paying special attention to the rim. You never knew where these mouths had been. She assumed the ice dispenser was broken considering a used condom hung from it. Using the cup, she scooped some ice from a cooler and topped her drink off with lemon-lime soda. A bonfire was roaring out back. She could see the flames dancing through the kitchen window.

*Kells said she'd be out here.*

Samantha passed by the hot tub, where boys were swapping stories from Spring Semester. They also wore frayed caps. These had bottle tops from imported beer strategically clamped down in a row along the bill. Their eyes followed her. She was accustomed to boys gawking at her, but it no longer held the same flattery as it did in high school. At this point in her life, it was downright creepy.

She followed a familiar aroma, walking down the home's two story deck. It was a nice home, built by someone's hedge fund parents. Lots of land, lots of amenities, and lots of marble. The hedge fund-sters thought it would be a good idea to leave their college kid home alone while they vacationed. Always a bad idea.

When Samantha made it to ground level, she saw a group of co-eds passing a joint back and forth. She took a sip from her cup and decided to make nice with them. If this was all the party had to offer, she'd better be high enough to at least make it interesting.

One guy had long hair. It was straight, sleek, and he reminded Samantha of Jesus. Jesus Hair wore a tie-dyed shirt with a yellow happy face in the middle of it. A joint was stuck in the corner of its mouth. 'Be Happy, Mon!' was printed below the happy face. And it certainly did look happy.

Jesus Hair held the joint up to Samantha as she approached him. He was restraining a cough, trying to keep the smoke in his lungs as long as possible. She took a long drag. Jesus Hair smiled and waved her on. She tipped her cup to him and continued across the plush, manicured lawn, taking small tokes from the joint as she headed toward the bonfire.

The moon hung above the roaring fire's heat like a thumbnail. It was sharp at each end, suspended against the dark canopy sky. Samantha gazed into the fire's wondrous heat, watching as flames changed colors. Blue, orange, white, red. Then it crackled, sending a chunk of hot ash onto her foot. It landed between the straps of her flip-flops. She casually brushed the ash off with her opposing foot, numb from the whiskey and weed.

Among the group surrounding the fire was a frail-looking man. He looked much older than everyone else. He wore his hat backwards, the bill free of decorative bottle caps. He strummed an acoustic guitar while the group nodded their heads in unison, hypnotized by the chords he played. He didn't look like Jesus Hair, but he was damn close.

*A modern day Charlie Manson maybe?*

She took visual inventory of everyone, squinting through the black smoke as it followed her, hoping to find her Kells. "Anyone seen my friend? Her name's Kelly. Dark hair." Holding her hand to her chin, "She's about yay high."

A guy with a terrible beard, overgrown and un-groomed, scratched his head. "Kelly? Um, yeah man. I think she left."

"Left? With who? Are you sure?"

He shrugged his shoulders. Samantha flicked the joint, now a roach, into the fire and sat down herself. The soft ground was damp against her skin. Her senses were elevating. She felt her heart beat against her tank-top while she massaged her feet through fine blades of grass. The pot had a strobe effect on her vision. Everything was breathing, especially the fire. It flickered a multitude of color—appearing, vanishing, pulsing.

She finished her drink and left an ice cube in her mouth to prevent it from drying out and sent Kelly a text message.

> I'm by the fire. Where are you slut?

She placed the phone on the flat of her stomach. It was too difficult to stuff it back into her cut-off jeans.

*I should feel it vibrate, right? I should see it illuminate, right? It's too much to think about right now. The buzz will wear off in a few hours. I'll just chill here for a while…*

———————————

When she woke up, Samantha was alone. The fire had gone out. The acoustic guitar Manson was strumming was leaning against a hay bale. She heard sporadic voices over classic rock music coming from the house. She checked her phone. A red exclamation point floated above the message icon, indicating that her text wasn't sent.

She touched her throbbing bladder, as it did when it was full, but she wasn't ready to sit up yet. Her head hung between still-a-little-buzzed and hungover. A small pain crept into her temples like a tiny pick-axe chipping away at an ice block. She massaged them with her fingers. This party was officially over.

Getting up, she maintained her balanced just enough to walk around a wood shed at the corner of the property. She didn't want to go inside the house just yet. There could've been a line. There could've been someone passed out on the floor. There could've been a lot of things. She just wanted to pee and leave quietly, to disappear into the night. She loosened her fly, pulled her shorts down, and squatted. Once she finished, she buttoned herself up and headed for the ashy remains of the bonfire where her phone and flip-flops still were. She would slip them on, walk around the house to avoid the remaining party people, slide into her car, and drive home. Then her mouth filled with saliva.

Putting her hands to her knees, Samantha released brown liquid from her mouth like tap water from a rusty garden hose. She coughed a few times, repeated, and then spat. Although she felt a little better, her nausea returned, full force.

This time, she buckled over on all fours, clenching the ground with her fists, white knuckling the grass. It felt like something was pulling at her intestines. Thick, yellow bile slid up her throat and plopped out of her mouth. She smacked the ground with a frustrated hand and rested her head on her arm. The fetal position was nice, for now. The metallic taste in her mouth was not.

She rested for what seemed like hours, trying to focus, trying to gather herself so she could drive home. She rubbed at her watery eyes, her vision distorted from warping a contact lens. There was a figure in the distant field. A figure too tall to be Kelly. A stalk of wheat hung from its mouth. The figure ceased where the tall grass ended and the property Samantha laid on began, tilting its head to the side, curious.

"Hey man," Samantha said. "Can you help me up?"

Samantha recognized the figure, a man, but just like the song from earlier, couldn't place from where. With an outstretched hand, she turned to him. The man knelt down next to her, ignoring the gesture, and cupped his tattooed hand over her mouth. He pinched Samantha's nose closed with the other hand and wrapped his legs around her waist, coiling like a snake. There was little struggle.

# 30

Daryl always followed the rules. No matter how strict, how asinine, he always toed the line. However, when it came to fishing at Pine View Park, Daryl lived by his own set of rules. First rule, catch and release. Never keep your fish as a trophy. Let it grow big for the next person. That way, you can share the same thrill. Second, always leave your fishing spot cleaner than you found it. This was hard to do because he was a light traveler, but there was always a glass bottle here, a sandwich wrapper there, that needed recycling. And third, you never tell anybody about your favorite fishing hole. Daryl found this one as a child, exploring the outskirts of town one day out of boredom. Not even his Grandpa Woody knew about it, that's how secret it was.

After walking the small trail through dense wilderness, Daryl saw the one lake, out of many here, that was his discovery. It wasn't as big as the other lakes, but it did yield the best action out of the other ones he had fished out of. It was also private, with tall pine trees providing a wall—a sense of security—from the world. He adjusted his trucker's cap and took in a deep breath, marveling at the lake's beauty.

He removed an earthworm from a carton with slotted holes. The worm was cold and firm between his fingers as he baited his hook. It twisted its body with precision. Daryl capped the tail end of the worm back to the pointed end of the hook, pulled his line taut, and casted it into the mirrored lake.

Daryl rested his pole against a Y-shaped branch that he found close to the embankment and rinsed the dirt off his hands in the cool water, shimming his way back through sticky grass, and sat on a log. Clouds moved in front of the blistering sun, providing temporary relief from its heat. A small breeze blew over the water, causing the cattails to arch slightly. Daryl was alone. The cicadas sang. It was a good day for freedom.

Daryl opened his tackle box and dug through lures, hooks, and bobbers, eventually finding a pouch of chewing tobacco. It wasn't habitual. It helped him relax. The sweet aroma tingled his nose hairs when he opened the package. He placed a chunk of it between his cheek and gum, pulled his hat down low over his eyes, and slumped down against the log. He began to think about the girl from his dream. The same one who was missing. *What was her name?* She played his harmonica without any practice, just like he had. But that didn't explain why it riled up the pigs so bad when she played it. *One weird dream, Daryl.* He began drifting off, when he heard a rustling in the grass behind him.

"Shit," a voice said. It was Sid. He wore a brown and yellow flannel shirt, the collar up. Daryl supposed this was to cover up the marks his dad left on his throat. He had on steel-toed boots. The usual flat billed hat was missing. A fishing pole rested on his shoulder.

"Ain't we seeing a lot of each other lately?" Sid said.

"Look," Daryl said, "I come here to think. So if you don't mind."

"Yeah, me too," Sid replied, walking along the edge of the lake. "Look man, thanks for your help last night. My dad's a real asshole, but I know he loves my mom and me. He's just stressed is all."

*He would've choked you to death if I hadn't been there. You and I both know it.*

Sid carefully tossed his lure between algae and logs that inhabited the lake. Daryl watched in amusement as Sid continued to cast and reel. He knew he wasn't going to catch anything over there. Maybe a snag at best.

"You're going to have a heck of a time catching anything over there without a kayak," Daryl said. "Over here is the best spot to fish without one. Figured you'd know that since you come here often."

Ignoring Daryl, Sid continued along the bank, plopping his lure into the water. Giving up, he reeled in his line and lit a cigarette. He glanced over in Daryl's direction, blew smoke through his nostrils, and spat in the water. Meanwhile, Daryl felt for his utility knife, making sure it within reach. Just in case.

"Your bobber's down!" Sid shouted.

Daryl stood up and grabbed his pole, giving it a tug to the right to set his hook. The reel whined as the fish tried to elude Daryl. He gave his line some slack so it wouldn't snap as the tip of his pole bent forward. The fish was swimming deeper. Keeping his weight centered, he reeled the line slowly, with patience, practically leading the fish in a dance of sorts. In one final attempt to break free from the capture, the fish jumped out of the water, glistening in the sun at a ninety-degree angle, flipped forward, then smacked its tail on the water's surface, propelling circular ripples of lake water around it.

"Hold on to it, man. I'm coming over!" said Sid. He crushed

the cigarette out on the bottom of his boot, dropped it into his flannel breast pocket, and shuffled through tall weeds to join Daryl.

"Je-sus Christ!" Daryl said. "This things a monster!"

"Just keep it steady and don't break the line!" Sid was now crawling toward the water. He rolled up his sleeves and slid down the embankment. Half of him in the water, the other half anchored to a tree root that twisted out of the ground. "Nice and easy, Daryl."

Sid plunged his arm into the lake, grabbed the bottom lip of the tired largemouth, and pulled it up. It flopped and wiggled, as if it were being electrocuted. Sid placed his hand on the underbelly while keeping his grip on the bass' mouth, raising it up high in victory. Its flesh was a forest-green and it cascaded into a seafoam that faded into its white belly.

"Goddam it. This is the biggest fish I've ever seen!" Sid said. "Eight pounds, at least!" He removed the hook and handed the fish to Daryl.

Daryl held the bass from its lower lip and let its body suspend in the air as he studied the length. Then he placed it in both of his hands and raised it slightly.

"Yeah, it's every bit of eight pounds," he said. "Not bad."

"Not bad?" Sid said, wiping his slimy hands on his jeans. "Dude that might be a record!"

"Yeah, well, nobody will ever know. We're not supposed to be back here."

"Fuck that. Say cheese!" Sid took a photo with his camera phone.

"Okay, damn, hold on. Let me get it in front of me. It'll look even bigger!" Daryl extended the fish away from his body and smiled. Sid snapped away.

"Perfect, man. Now you know you have to kiss it before you release it. It's bad luck if you don't."

"I. Am. Not. Kissing. This. Fish." Daryl said.

"It's easy. Look." Sid put his mouth between the round eyes of the bass and smacked his lips against its slippery scales. Then, in disgust, he said, "See? That wasn't so bad!"

"Yeah. I'll take your word for it." He placed the fish into the water and moved it around to wake it up. The bass started to regain its energy. Its tail swayed back and forth before it shot forward and disappeared into the murky water.

"Let's celebrate!" Sid removed a joint from a crumpled cigarette pack.

"I don't smoke," Daryl said. "It's bad on the lungs."

Sid lit it. "This is a time of peace, between you and me. An ancient ritual between the Indians and our forefathers. Just one hit. It won't kill you."

"I won't go psycho?"

"Maybe a little."

Daryl inhaled. It burned his lungs and made his nose itch, but he was determined to hold it in, just as Sid had before passing it to him.

"Not bad, huh?" Sid said. "But you have to blow the smoke out."

Daryl exhaled. Saliva strung from his mouth. His eyes watered. In between coughs, "Not bad at all, thanks."

Sid laid his back against the log and folded his arms behind his head. He passed the joint back to Daryl and watched the puffy clouds hover in the sky. "I come here mostly just to get away from home. I'm not nearly the sportsman you are." He lit another cigarette and blew a cloud of smoke into the air. "I can't wait to get out of this place. How about you? Do you have any plans on leaving since schools out?"

"I'll probably stick around, help my Grandpa with the farm. It'll be mine one day. Don't need college for that."

"Good for you, man. Not me. I want to go somewhere, somewhere BIG, like New York City. That's where the real action is. Not here. Not in this trap. That's what happens you know. You grow up in a small town, with small people who have small ideas, and live small lives.

"What's wrong with that?"

"Nothing, I guess. But it ain't for me, man. Fuck this place." Sid turned to Daryl, who was studying his hand and wiggling his fingers.

"How you feel?"

"Like I'm dreaming."

Sid laughed. "Yeah, this shit will do that to ya. Hey, tell me something about that harmonica of yours."

"Like what?"

"Like how you can play it so good."

"I just can," Daryl said, shrugging his shoulders.

"Really? Because we tried to play it. All of us. It didn't do shit. Didn't even make a sound."

"Well maybe it won't play for assholes. Works for me just fine."

"Maybe it doesn't. I was an asshole. Sorry about that. You did get Flint good though. He cried in the truck. It was pretty funny. We gave him a bunch of shit for it."

Daryl smiled.

"We cool, D? I'm not saying we got to be bestie's or anything." He held his fist out. Daryl bumped it.

"Yeah. You're alright, D."

# 31

Margaret whistled playfully, dancing along to a record player as it spun music from the Big Band Era. She ran a synthetic duster across black and white family photographs set in simple framework. The expressions on the faces were bleak, almost angry. The adults held various farm tools, while the children held crooked sticks. She paid one photo special attention. A woman laced in a white doily dress, her mouth as stiff as wood. She was holding a baby. Margaret shined this picture using her spit and elbow.

"We going to make you so proud, Momma. Just you wait and see."

Next, she pulled back thick Victorian curtains to clean the windows. A cloud of dirt formed around a police car, a white Crown Vic, as it rolled down the driveway, toward the house.

"Get in the basement!" she warned. "We got company!"

Jud walked into the living room, nibbling at an ear of corn.

"Get away from the windows you big dumb idiot. It's the law!"

His head perked up, curious if she was fibbing, and peeked around her as the police car came to a stop. Disgusted, he spat corn on the floor.

"I just mopped in here," she said. "Get your ass down there!"

"Fuck the law, sis," he said as he approached the basement door. "I ain't scared of 'em."

Samantha blinked her eyes awake. Her head was spinning. *I must be hungover.* She turned her head, trying to figure out where she was, which she often did after a good night out. Once things came into "one contact lens focus", she realized three things. One, she was in a basement. Two, her hands were tied. And three, she was now looking at the end of a five-pointed pitchfork.

"I'm the Pig Man," Jud said. "And if you scream, I'll stab you real good." Jud wore a rubber pig mask. The ears long. The smile demented as it spread inside rows of wrinkled curves that stretched to two eyelets. It's long, twisted snout and crooked plastic teeth flopped about when he spoke.

Samantha gasped. She saw a little girl sunk behind one of the many burlap sacks that were scattered along the basement floor. Her face was dirty and swollen, her hair knotted from the neglect of daily hygiene. She met the girl's eyes. They reminded her of a feral child, lost in the woods. The girl covered her eyes and slowly went back into hiding.

There was a knock at the front door, followed by the ding-dong of a doorbell. It was an odd sound, the doorbell—the kind a butler would respond to.

Margaret checked her faux smile several times in the mirror before greeting the police officers. She ran her fingers through her graying hair, trying to decide if she should leave it up or down. She decided to leave it down. There was an innocence about her when it was.

"Why, good afternoon officers," she said, and immediately

corrected herself after she saw the sheriff's badge. "I mean officer and *sheriff*."

"Afternoon, ma'am. I'm Sheriff Mills and this man here behind me is Deputy Wolfe. Sorry to bother you on such a beautiful day but we were wondering if we could ask you a few questions."

Wolfe careened around Mills, careful not to step on the many cats that occupied the porch, and attempted to get a glimpse inside the house. Noticing his curiosity, Margaret pulled the door closer to the jamb.

"Questions about what?" she asked.

Mills removed the khaki brimmed hat that rested above his aviators and wiped the sweat clean from his forehead with a handkerchief. "It's awful hot out here..." Mills said, unsure of how to finish the sentence because Margaret never introduced herself.

"Oh, where are my manners? Margaret. Name's Margaret."

"Well Margaret. It's blazing out here. Would you mind if we spoke inside?"

She shifted her eyes to the side and chuckled. "I'm afraid it's hotter in this old farmhouse than it is out there. My, do you think I have central air conditioning?"

"No, I guess you wouldn't."

Margaret glanced at Wolfe who was now walking around to the side of the house. He returned shortly after, hands in pockets, inspecting the property line. She didn't take her eyes off him.

"How about we step inside and talk, just for a moment?"

"Oh dear sheriff, this place is a pigsty. I wouldn't want ya'll coming in here thinking I was some sort of slob."

"We won't," Mills said bluntly. He was growing tired of the cute back and forth banter. He could tell Margaret was hiding something, and she wasn't going to let him find out what it was.

"Like he said, we just want to ask you a few questions," said Wolfe, shooing away more of the mangy cats.

"Honey, I already answered all the questions you asked me. Now, if you'll excuse me."

Mills stuck his black leather boot in the doorway as she tried to close the door on him. Her kind, country smile quickly turned to a scowl.

"A little girl went missing here a few days ago. You know anything about that?"

Margaret kept her eyes on his boot.

"Answer the question and I'll move it."

"What makes you think I know something about that? Because I live here all by myself, all alone with nobody to keep me company besides my kittens?" Then she pointed at the officers. "You guys have your precious little town with your precious little people to look out for. And they was the ones who pushed my family out. I know I'm not welcome there and they ain't welcome here and that's fine by me. You should have the same respect, coming down here, harassing me and all." Her eyes darted back and forth, from Mills to Wolfe, then back again, her reflection in his sunglasses staring back at her. Mills removed his boot.

"You don't think I know about the rumors ya'll spread about my bloodline? Our legacy? Ya'll are disgusting and you ain't welcome here. That said, do you have a warrant?"

Mills shook his head. Margaret showed him her rotting

teeth and scrunched her eyebrows. "Then get the hell off my property!" She slammed the door shut. Mills and Wolfe looked at each other, then glanced at the front door.

"That went all kinds of well," Wolfe said, as they left the porch and walked back to the police car.

"You buy it?" Mills said.

"Buy what? That she's some kind of old witch who was banished by the town? Absolutely! Did you see her? She looks like someone fucked a ragdoll and left it out to dry. She's nuts."

Mills took one last look at the old farmhouse. It hadn't seen a coat of paint in decades and the roof was sunk in by the crumbling chimney. It seemed like hundreds of cats were crawling on top of one another on the wrap around porch. One cat in particular was licking itself on the rickety porch swing. To the left-rear of the farmhouse was a metal corral. Empty. Its rusted railings were warped, not from something like hail damage, but from something else. Something much stronger, like a small tractor tried to drive straight through them.

He placed his brimmed hat back on his head and removed the aviators from his face. Squinting, he focused on the upstairs window. Somebody was peeking at him between the curtains. It was Margaret.

"Yeah, but crazy don't mean she's guilty."

"Don't mean she's innocent neither," replied Wolfe.

———————

Margaret came rushing down the basement staircase. Jud still had the pitchfork hovering above Samantha. "Get that thing out of her face! I'm going to make sure there ain't nothing outside to bring suspicion on us. Keep them two quiet!"

Jud grunted through the mask and, with the pitchfork, stuck the bag that Penny was hiding behind. He motioned her to join Samantha, who embraced her as she held those little tethered hands.

He squealed quietly, his voice muffled through the rubber walls of the mask. His hand fell between his legs and he started rubbing himself through his jeans.

"Don't even think about it, asshole," Samantha warned. She wanted to scream it, grab him by those curly pig ears and yell it right it in his face. But it only came out as a whisper.

He adjusted the mask and held the pitch fork against his shoulder, protecting himself from some imaginary threat. "The Pig Man don't like loud noise. Make his ears hurt. And when his ears hurt, he get mad. When he get mad, he get dangerous. He don't like trespassers neither. But you're okay. You ain't tresspassin'. We brought you here, so you can be with us. So we can be a family. You'll see, it'll be real nice."

Margaret returned holding Samantha's cell phone and flip-flops. "You won't be needing these anymore," she said. "Well, I suppose you can keep the sandals, if you're a good girl."

Penny noticed that Margaret could be wearing the same dress she had on when she first met her. Judging from the stains of dried sweat that covered it, Penny concluded that Margaret hadn't removed it since.

Margaret clapped her hands together then placed them on her hips as she exhaled. "Whew, that was close. Could've been ugly." She patted Jud on the head and massaged her fingers against the pale rubber. His head shook as he grunted and snorted. Then he grabbed Margaret by her ass.

"Look at this, Penelope," Margaret said, tilting her head like an adoring mother. "Looks like we found you a big sister. Someone you can look up to."

"One big happy family," Jud said. Then he playfully ran the pitchfork over Margaret's legs, scraping dead skin off of them. With a flirtatious laugh, she ran her hand under her dress. Penny nestled her head into Samantha's chest as Jud squealed, chasing his sister back up the stairs.

"What's your name?" Penny asked, as Samantha stroked the dirt out of the little girl's hair.

"Samantha."

"You can call me Penny. All my friends do."

Samantha cupped Penny's face and turned it toward her. "Okay, Penny. "We're going to get out of here. Do you understand?"

Penny grabbed Samantha's wrists. Her eyebrows raised. A hint of hope began to emerge through the young girl's fragile eyes as Samantha continued.

"I saw your picture at the grocery store I work at. I think the cops were just here too. They're on to those two."

"Why didn't they come down here and get us?" Penny asked, raising her voice.

Samantha put her finger to Penny's parted lips. "Because that woman lied to them. But the cops will be back. We just have to play along with them, earn their trust. Then we'll make a run for it."

"How long will that be?"

"Soon."

"Promise?"

She touched Penny's nose, "I promise."

# 32

Brad placed a plug into each ear. A traditional target, the silhouette of a man, hung fifty-feet away from him. A numbered scoring system encircled different areas on the figure. The number seven was just on the inside of the target, right around where the ribs would be. Numbers eight and nine were closer to the center of the body. Finally, there was number ten, dead center. Bulls-eye.

A solemn look came over Brad as he raised the revolver, a snub nosed .38 special hand gun that travelled with him from the city. He had done enough research to know that when it came to weaponry, monsters weren't biased. He could almost see through the target and the wall behind it, blocking out the other marksmen working on their accuracy. He had no feeling, no emotion. This was the look of a madman. Because of his research, he knew this to be true.

The first six rounds fired in succession. The first five missed. The sixth hit the shoulder. He reloaded. Four out of his next six shots hit the chin area. He took a deep breath, held it for a moment, and then exhaled. His shooting was sloppy. He had to knock the rust off. He needed to focus.

The next round tore through the target, again in the shoulder. He aimed for the heart, the big red oval, but instead put one in the number nine zone. A broken rib. The third shot landed above the shoulder. The next two spliced the paper target in the groin area. *Getting closer.*

He thought of Penny and raised the gun with steady form and fired the last bullet. It split the right side of the target's oblong head. *Splattered brains on the wall.* Using a lever, he moved the target toward him to inspect the damage. He tore if off the metal clip, crumpled it up, and replaced it with another. He had two boxes of ammo. It was going to be a long night.

# 33

*Daryl. Wake up.*

Samantha took Daryl by the head and caressed his cheek. He opened his eyes. Her long, blonde hair draped over her shoulder, slightly covering his face. She smiled. Her teeth aligned in a perfect row, a divine curve. He sat up. Standing above him, she now held a swaddled baby. This didn't feel right.

"Why do you have a baby?"

"I don't know how much longer I'll be able to keep her safe. We're really scared and you must save us. You must save us from the Pig Man."

She placed the baby on the ground. It crawled away into the shadows. A loud click echoed through the dark space, followed by a light, a spotlight, showcasing Samantha, wearing nothing but her undergarments. Her skin was covered with long, thin slashes, as if she were struck by a switch. He couldn't take his eyes off of them.

"They hurt, Daryl."

Samantha pointed to a window on the east side of the room. Daryl levitated toward it. Looking through, the sky was angry. A shot of thunder exploded. A bolt of lightning cracked across the dark atmosphere and when it did, he saw a metal corral slightly to the left of an old farmhouse. A sounder of pigs fought, ripping their skin off each other. Huge chunks of bloody pig flesh flung in the air as they cannibalized themselves.

A figure emerged in the distance and, approaching the sty, stabbed at the snorting pigs through the railings with a pitchfork—keeping them riled up, ensuring they mutilated each other. The figure's head leaned back, a satisfying gesture, and laughter rolled out of its mouth. A haunted warning.

"Hurry back, Daryl. She's coming!"

When Daryl turned around, he saw that Samantha was now fully clothed and Penny was pointing at a staircase next to her. He charged up the stairs. The door to the basement opened just before he reached the top step. Margaret was standing in the doorway. Her skin was stretched thin across her skeletal frame. She was holding a text book and a yard stick covered with thick, dried paint. Black.

"You…you….sinner!" Margaret screamed. The muscles in her neck pulled taut with each word. She cracked Daryl across the face with the yard stick. He wet himself.

"Stay away from my family!" she said, swiping at his face again, missing only by inches. Her teeth were razor sharp. Her gray hair flecked with red floated above her, ignoring gravity, as she backed Daryl down the staircase.

He quickly met Samantha and Penny, who were pointing at his pocket. He reached into it and removed his harmonica. Margaret's arm extended to a great length and knocked it out of his hand. He was paralyzed from an unknown force, unable to reach it. Margaret was now in his face. Her breath was disgusting.

"How you going to save them now, sheepfucker?"

---

Daryl sat up. It took him a moment to catch his breath. Confused, he searched for something he could recognize, hoping this wasn't another nightmare. Then he saw his harmonica. It was next to his alarm clock, right where he had left it. He pulled the covers over his head with trembling hands and tried not to think, tried not to dream.

# 34

The first thing Daryl noticed when he arrived to Jimbo's Market the following morning was a large news van parked by the entrance. A satellite dish was positioned at the top-rear corner, entangled by large, black cables. He watched as overweight men wearing Channel 4 News baseball caps bustled about. Some carried heavy cameras, others carried steel boxes.

A few feet from the van was a thin, attractive woman. She was a brunette with eyebrows cropped above blue eyes. Her lips were perfectly spaced below her slender nose. Makeup was being applied to her face as she spoke in a fluid rhythm to a man half her age while he took notes.

Jimbo was behind her. He had a dour twist to his mouth. His posture loose, defeated.

She dismissed the note taker and makeup artist with urgency.

"Rubber baby buggy bumpers."

"Rubber baby buggy bumpers."

She repeated those lines until a hefty man with a camera held up his hand and counted down to zero with his fingers.

"I'm Tina O'Brien with Channel Four News. The sudden disappearance of eight year old Penelope Carter has left the rural town of Edlund stunned. Now, with twenty year old Samantha Swanson missing, people in the community are demanding answers."

Tina took several steps back, putting Jimbo in the camera's frame.

"Here with me now is owner of Jimbo's Market, Mr. James Davis. Tell me Mr. Davis, when was the last time you saw Samantha Swanson?"

Hand in pocket, Jim reluctantly answered, avoiding eye contact with the camera. "Well, Samantha is a good, honest person. It's not like her to not show up for work. I mean she's never done that. Never called in sick or anything."

"Do you think the person responsible for this is the same person responsible for the disappearance of Penelope Carter?"

"Um, I really don't know."

"Tell me Mr. Davis, was Samantha ever…"

Before Tina could finish, Mills slammed the brakes on his Crown Vic. He hopped out of the car, engine running, and left the door open behind him. He approached her with an accusing finger.

"You!" he shouted, pointing. "Shut this down!"

"I'm just asking the good people of this town about the disappearance of Ms. Swanson. If you'd been doing your job, I wouldn't have to be here."

"I am doing my job, Tina. I'm warning you. Tell that guy to shut the camera off or I will arrest you for impeding on my investigation."

Ignoring him, Tina continued. "Sheriff Mills is here with us. Sheriff, I'd like to ask you a few questions regarding the two missing person's reports on your desk."

"Get that goddam camera out of my face. I warned you once and I'm not going to do it again." Mills removed his handcuffs.

Smirking, Tina continued to hold the microphone's position. "You can't do this you know, shut us down." Then, glancing at the cuffs, "Or arrest us."

He leaned into her. "You want me to find those girls? Stop bothering these people. I probably already have one vigilante on my hands. I don't need more."

Tina looked at the cuffs, then back to Mills.

"Shut it off, Marv."

Mills took Jimbo inside. Daryl watched the news team pack their gear. Tina had a cigarette in her right hand. She was shouting into her cellphone at someone in her left. "No. We didn't find anything. Barney Fife shut us down. Yeah, okay." She hung up and spotted Daryl. "Hey, you!"

Daryl looked around, confused, and pointed to himself.

"Yes, you! Do you work here with Samantha?"

He nodded.

"Can you tell me when you last saw her?"

Daryl could see Mills and Jimbo through the market's windows that had sale items written on them with wet marker. Judging by the look on Mills' face, the conversation wasn't going well for Mr. James Davis.

"No, ma'am," Daryl said, as he hurried inside.

Tina wrinkled her nose and mocked him. "No ma'am," she said, and crushed the cigarette with her heel.

---

Daryl stamped his time card and looked over at register seven, Samantha's register. It was closed and had been for days. His heart sank. She was the one who touched his hand. The one who saw him perform. She was the one who cared. Now she was gone and he was going to do something about it. Little did he know, he was the only one who could.

# 35

After Daryl's shift that day, it was a slow one without Samantha to help pass the time (Tina's intrusion didn't help either), he arrived at the police station. Mills was pouring coffee into his "I'm Buck" mug.

"You got to believe me, Sheriff," Daryl said. "I'm telling you. She's at that old pig farm off 83."

"Son, we done told you. There isn't anyone there but a lonely woman and her cats. Now, if you'll excuse me, I have some important work to do, in case you didn't notice." He brushed Daryl aside and sat at his desk. Wolfe, meanwhile, continued typing away at his computer, an old desktop version with a large monitor. Mills slid his reading glasses down the bridge of his nose behind a stack of papers, looking up at Daryl with his head lowered.

"Son. Why are you still here?"

"Why don't you believe me? Do you think I'm slow or something?"

Mills removed his glasses and chuckled. "Do I think you're slow? Daryl, I've known your family my entire life. Hell, they even voted me in as sheriff, remember? You're good people, like most of the folks here. But you have to trust me when I tell you that we've been to the farm. Me and Deputy Wolfe."

Daryl glanced over at Wolfe, now leaning back in his office chair. He nodded.

"Besides, we don't have any probable cause. I can't just go busting the door down on a hunch."

"She's in the basement, with that little girl whose face is all over town. Did you check the basement?"

"And yet you're still here and you still keep saying that. So, I'm supposed to go to the county judge and ask for a warrant based on some nightmare you had?" Mills adjusted himself upright. "Um, excuse me, judge? Can I have a warrant so I can search an old farmhouse based on a young man's dream? Yes? Well alright then! Thank you." He leaned over his desk and returned the glasses to his face. "Now what kind of sense does that make?"

"None, I guess."

"You guess right. It doesn't make any sense at all. You know what I am going to do? I'm going to tell you this one thing only because you seem to care so much about her."

Mills reclined in his chair, crossed his legs, and propped them on the corner of his desk. He folded his hands together, opening and closing them as he spoke.

"Truth is Daryl, Samantha could be anywhere. She didn't get along with her parents. Her grades were bad and, like most people her age, she liked to party. These dreams you're having are probably just your head trying to make sense of it. People up and go all the time, change their names and start new lives. But, if you ask me, she probably went on one of them 'dope journeys' to find herself."

Wolfe stood up and escorted Daryl to the door.

"Please leave this investigation up to the professionals and go back to living your life? Please?"

Daryl hung his head and left.

"Kid thinks he's a real Hardy Boy."

"Yes he does, sheriff," Wolfe said, typing away again.

"What in the hell got you so busy over there on your typing machine?"

"Doing the reports," he said, shrugging his shoulders. "Just like you asked me too."

"I want you at that farm tonight. Overnight watch. And keep your radio on. So much as a mouse hiccups out there, I better know about it."

"Do you think the boy's going to the farm?"

Mills ran his forefinger and thumb through his bushy mustache. "I don't know what to think anymore. But we don't need anybody getting hurt. I wouldn't be surprised if old Margaret doesn't have a shotgun loaded somewhere."

"You think Pig Man will get Daryl or Mr. Carter, don't you?"

"Goddam it, Wolfe. Just do what I ask. Okay?" Mills took a sip from his coffee mug. "You know you're being insubordinate when you question my orders."

---

Outside, Daryl went straight to the nearest payphone after exiting through the double doors of the police station. He opened the complimentary phone book and flipped through its pages until he found a name. Brisco Farley, Sid's dad. He placed a quarter in the slot and dialed the number. It rang for some time. Daryl pictured Brisco passed out on his easy chair, too inebriated to get up. After twelve or so rings, an irritated voice finally came through on the other end.

"What?"

"Um. Is Sid home? I'd like to talk to him please."

"And who the hell is this?"

"My name's Daryl, sir. I'm a friend from school."

There was a pause, a snort, and a belch. "Ha! You're lying. My boy ain't got no friends."

Daryl tried to make out the song that was playing in the background. It was either Eddie Money or Billy Squire, he couldn't tell which because of the dog barking in the background. Poor Rusty would probably get it good for this.

"Hold on," Brisco said. "Sidney! Phone!"

"Yeah?" came Sid's voice on the other end.

"Sid. It's Daryl. I need your help."

# 36

For Diana, it all happened in a blur. There was a rapping at the door, followed by Brad's flailing arms as he shouted at Mills and Wolfe. Then there was the whiskey later on in the day. Some mumbling. She tried to calm him down by rubbing his neck, shoulders, and back. It didn't work. His mind was made up.

Brad told her to stay put. As if she had a choice with only one good leg and no vehicle. He was holding his revolver in a leather gloved hand. She asked him to think it through while he loaded it. One in the barrel and six in the chamber. Seven shots. Lucky number seven. If the sheriff wasn't going to find his daughter, then he was.

# 37

Wolfe arrived to the farmhouse just before nightfall. He parked on a gravel path that led to a cornfield, his favorite spot to clock speeding vehicles. He poured coffee from his thermos and waited for someone to either enter or exit the property adjacent from him.

---

Brad decided it was best to take the half-mile hike up SR 83 on foot after parking his car by an old ravine. This way, he could better avoid the chance of being spotted by anyone. He checked his revolver and started toward the old farmhouse. The brush wasn't too thick to wade through and it provided him with enough cover from the road to go unnoticed by an occasional passerby.

---

Daryl met Sid at their hidden lake.

Sid unzipped a duffle bag when Daryl arrived. "Okay, D. Here's what we got." He removed each weapon as he identified them. "Crowbar, brass knuckles, bowie knife, ninja star." Then he removed a red stick. "One piece of dynamite."

"What the hell, Sid? Dynamite?"

"I don't even know if it works, man. I found it in my Dad's pile of junk out back. I just figured, what the hell, you know?"

"Yeah, who knows? Maybe we'll blow the place to smithereens!"

They laughed away their nervousness and pulled balaclava's over their faces. After bumping their bare knuckles together, they headed through the brush. Daryl led the way, clearing branches and snapping twigs. Sid had the unfortunate luck of being behind him, dodging thorny branches as they swung at him like a spring-loaded door. Just a minor inconvenience to the follower.

———————————

Three hours in and Wolfe already felt sleepy, despite the coffee he had been sipping. He wondered if he brewed decaf by mistake. He looked over each shoulder to make sure nobody was watching and removed his smart phone. He swiped his finger several times and started a movie that he downloaded earlier that day, right after Mills gave the order.

# 38

Draping to the floor from Margaret's hand was a small leather whip. She let the frayed tassels fall through her fingers while she caressed them, admiring its craftsmanship. Her horrible smile quickly turned to a frown and she reached her scabby arm back, and struck Samantha across her face with the whip.

"Sinner!" she yelled. Her face became distorted when she said the word. She snapped the whip again, cracking open Samantha's soft, tan legs. They didn't bleed at first. That would come later after the numbness from the lashings wore off.

"You fucking bitch!" Samantha screamed. The tears that rolled down her face were out of anger, not pain. Mucous bubbled from her left nostril. Penny was behind her with her hands over her ears. Eyes closed.

"Blasphemy! You little whore. I'll make sure those boys never want to touch you again!" Margaret twirled the whip above her head like a cowboy rounding up steer. Samantha covered her face behind her knees, her wrists still bound together. Margaret sent her arm forward. Penny climbed over Samantha. The whip caught her in the face and neck. She moaned, stunned by how powerful the blow was, and sent an ear-splitting shriek that echoed through the basement.

Jud scampered down the staircase.

"You're going to get it now, girlies," Margaret said.

Jud entered the basement holding the rubber pig mask and a steak knife. Chunks of bloody beef notched in its blade.

He held Samantha by her chin and licked the slashes on her cheek, running the dirty knife across her neck. "Mm, I've been wondering what you taste like."

Samantha opened her eyes. Jud looked familiar, but she couldn't quite place him until she saw the serpent tattoo on his hand. "It's you! The guy from the band."

Jud smiled and pulled the mask over his face. He hunched his back and grunted at Penny.

"Not her! Get the other one!" Margaret said. She cracked the whip across his back. He arched his shoulders, enjoying the sting as he placed his hands and knees down on the concrete floor. Samantha scurried against the wall, dragging the chain with her. The wall was cold against her back, almost comforting. Margaret snapped the whip again, this time across Jud's ass.

"Sic her, brother. *Sic her!*"

Jud placed his masked head on Samantha's bloody neck. His breath permeated below the snout, warming her skin. It was sensual for him. Terrifying for her. She began to cry.

Margaret grabbed Penny by each side of her head and made her watch as Jud ran his finger along Samantha's shoulder, down her side, and across her bleeding leg. "This is your fault. All you had to do was pay attention in class. But, no. You had to be a Stupid, didn't you? We give you a big sister and all you do is sass, sass, sass." Then, in a whisper, "Now you will watch as your sister accepts her punishment."

Jud unbuckled his jeans. Samantha struggled, trying to wrestle her hands free from the strong fiber that bound them. She whimpered and kicked her feet in the air. Jud flipped her over and drug a feed bag on top of her back as she wiggled around, trying to get free.

"Get her, brother, get her…"

Before she could finish encouraging her brother, Penny leaped at Margaret and bit down on her wrist. Her jaw mauled threw flesh and vein as blood squirted from her arm. Penny didn't let go. Margaret released her hands from Penny's head and tried to pull her arm away, forcing the tissue in her arm to stretch out like Silly Putty.

Jud turned around, rubber snout and all. He found Margaret holding her wrist with gory meat dangling between her fingers. He wrapped her in his arms.

"Get off me!" Margaret said. "These little sinners MUST BE PUNISHED FOR THEIR SINS!"

Penny spit a chunk of Margaret's arm onto the cold basement floor and pushed the feed bag off Samantha. She looked into her now hopeful eyes as they shifted between her legs. The steak knife. Penny put the knife in Samantha's hands. Space was tight, but there was enough room for Penny to place her tied hands over the blade. She rubbed the twine against it while Samantha held the handle tight.

Jud ignored Margaret's plea to leave her alone. He held her, rubbing the snout all over her neck like she was his wounded young. Then he tore the sleeve off his denim shirt and wrapped it around the gash in her skin.

"I'll need stitches, baby," she said. "I can sew myself up."

Penny continued to saw the rope against the knife, praying it would snap and break her free. Suddenly, a beam of light began dancing on the basement floor through the east-side basement window, the same window Penny gazed through before Samantha arrived.

The light caught Jud through the gaping holes of the pig mask. He ran up to the window. A figure wandered in the pasture by the house, holding a flashlight, the source for his distraction while he nurtured his sister.

"Who is it?" Margaret asked.

Jud shrugged his shoulders.

"Get the shotgun. Make sure they don't come inside."

When the twine finally split, Penny almost yelped. But she didn't. Samantha grabbed Penny's hands, as if they were still tied together. Penny didn't understand why.

"I'm going to take care of this," Margaret said, holding her arm that was wrapped with denim cloth, now stained in a black hue. She seemed dizzy, disorientated. "Whoever is out there is as good as dead. Now where is my..."

"Now, Penny!" Samantha shouted.

Penny snapped the whip against Margaret's veined legs. The tethers wrapped around them, gripped them, like they wanted her. Needed her. Penny looked like a deranged cannibal. Blood streaked against her chin, teeth red, as she cracked away at Margaret's pale limbs. They now looked like a barber shop pole, white laced with a swirling red. Margaret finally fell to the floor from the pain. It was too much.

Using leverage from the burlap sacks, Samantha managed to slide herself upright. Penny took the knife and freed Samantha's ankles. Now mobile, Samantha used the heel of her foot to stomp on the back of Margaret's head. She rolled Margaret over and sent her heel into her nose. It split open and spread across her cheek bones, sending red fluid into the air, a mist of cherry red.

"Now my hands. Hurry!"

Penny cut Samantha's hands free. She wrapped her little arms around Samantha's waist as Margaret's body lay sprawled out on the floor.

"One last thing."

Samantha thought she heard something jingle earlier. She turned her head and reached into the top of Margaret's dress and was careful not to accidentally brush her hand against anything in particular. Resting in her bosom was a key ring. Samantha used it to unlock Penny from the coiled chains.

"Is somebody here to save us?"

"I think so, sweetie."

Then they heard the blast of a shotgun.

# 39

Movie credits rolled across the screen of Wolfe's smartphone when the buckshot fired. He reached for the CB receiver, still shaken up from being awoke by the blast, and radioed Mills through a static airwave.

WOLFE: Sheriff, I heard a shot. Twelve-gauge. I'm going in. Copy.

MILLS: Not without me you're not. Stay put. I'm on my way. Copy.

WOLFE: But someone could be s-s-s-seriously hurt. C-c-copy.

MILLS: I'll be there in five. You're no good to anyone if you're dead. Copy.

WOLFE: R-r-roger that.

Wolfe quietly pulled his car out from the nook in the cornfield and parked along the edge of Margaret's house. He removed the shotgun from the dashboard of his police car. He cocked the action back to make sure it was loaded. It was. He took in deep, slow breaths to calm himself. He glanced into the rearview. Two separate circles of light bounced up and down through the brush that led to the farmhouse. He ran his fingers through his stiff hairline.

*Shit. What do I do? Sheriff told me to wait. "You're no good to anyone dead." Five minutes is too long. What if the boy was right? What if the crazy old bat shot someone? I have to find out who pulled that trigger.*

Wolfe made the sign of the cross across his body. *Of the Father, and of the son, and of the Holy Spirit.* He kissed his hand, pointed to the sky, and followed the dancing lights.

---

Ominous, gray clouds hung below the summer moon. Daryl and Sid crouched behind an oak tree, their shadows stretched across the pasture. All was quiet until the booming echo of buckshot reverberated through the air.

"That was a shotgun," Sid said. "We seriously brought a knife to a gunfight."

Daryl placed his finger to Sid's mouth. "Listen. Do you hear that?"

The twisting sound of metal was heard in the distance. Sid pointed his flashlight in the direction of the noise, trying to find its source. The light found the metal corral. It was vibrating, a rigorous clamor, as it filled itself with a sounder of atrocious swine. Sharp tusks erected from their mouths. Little red and brown hairs covered their muscular bodies. One in particular had beady yellow eyes. It seemed to command the others.

"Oh my God," Daryl said, as Sid just gazed in amazement.

Just like in Daryl's dream, hundreds of pigs began chomping and piling over one another as blood sprayed in random areas above the corral. The pig with the yellow eyes emerged from the ruckus, transforming into a tall figure. The figure beat its chest and bellowed as it waded through the massacre and climbed over the rusted railing.

This was the Pig Man. Two gnarly teeth protruded from his black gum line. A clear fluid drained from his pudgy nose that raised outward between two miserable eyes. Above those bleak eyes, a straw hat. It was frayed across the brim. Soiled overalls covered his potbelly. His skin, hairless. No eyebrows. No hair hung from his underarms. Just pale, rolling tides of skin. He scanned the pasture, looking for an intruder.

"Kill your light, Sid."

The two boys laid on their stomachs and watched through binoculars as the Pig Man opened the corral gate. The sounder tramped from their prison, freed by the Pig Man. They were thirsty for blood.

"Where did that thing come from, D?"

"The ground? Thin air? Same place those piggies came from?"

"What do we do now?"

"I dunno," Daryl said, tapping his nervous fingers on top of the binoculars.

While the boys were trying to figure out their next step of action, the front door of the farmhouse sprung open. Daryl nudged Sid and they panned their view to the front porch.

"Holy shit, it's Samantha!"

Samantha's long legs carried her across the wooden planks below her feet. Penny was behind her, following with outstretched arms. Samantha turned around, ready to catch her.

"You can make it, Penny! Jump down the stairs!"

Penny felt something tug at her back. It was Margaret's bloody arm. She wound Penny's cotton dress with her fist and pulled her backward.

"You little bitch! Get back here!"

Samantha lunged forward and grasped Penny's hands.

Determined to win this battle of tug-of-war, she sank her heels into the soft ground and leaned her body back as far as possible without falling over. Penny kicked and screamed, trying to elude Margaret's hold. Margaret pulled harder, ripping Penny's dress and sending her into her chest. Penny's foot fell into Margaret's mouth, toes and all. Margaret gagged. Penny removed her foot and stomped on Margaret's glossy eye. She felt a *pop!* as the eye collapsed into her skull.

"Girls, get over here!" shouted Wolfe. They took shelter behind him, avoiding the many dead cats that littered the front yard—their bodies stiff, hairs on end, like quills—and felt safe as he kept the end of his shotgun pointed at the haggard woman.

Jud came racing around the house with his mask on, not noticing the ghostly figure in overalls. "Hold it," commanded Wolfe, now aiming at Jud. He froze. Not from the shotgun that was pointing at him, but from Pig Man. He grabbed Jud by the throat and raised him several feet off the ground. He sniffed at Jud's mask, rubbing his snout into each crevice and fold, leaving behind a trail of slimy residue. A thick, black tongue flopped violently out of Pig Man's mouth and lapped up the slime. He turned his head, as if he was unimpressed, and began eating Jud's neck. Jud removed the mask, unable to scream, and kicked his legs about while Pig Man devoured his vocal chords.

"Dude, what the fuck?" said Sid.

"That's Jud. He's in this band I play, used, to play with. Son of a bitch kidnapped Samantha."

"Cops are here, dude. Look."

Red and blue lights pulsed across the wooden canopy that

surrounded the farmhouse. Before joining his deputy with the rescued victims, Mills checked his revolver. Locked and loaded.

Pig Man slung Jud's body over his shoulder. Jud's head hung askew. His eyes open with surprise. He mouthed something as blood spewed from his neck. Nobody would ever know what those words were because when Pig Man dropped him to the ground, a row of pigs lined up in a neat little row to feed from his body.

Margaret arose. She was on her hands and knees, now splintered with wood. She lifted her head, covering her right eye with her good hand and pointing at Penny with her mangled arm. "This is all your fault! You made this happen, sinners!" Saliva flew from her mouth when she spoke. Pig Man stood still, deciding who to go for next. A line of pigs behind him. Wolfe kept his aim.

"Freeze!" Mills said. "I don't know what kind of circus this is, but you make one more move and we'll shoot." He was pointing his gun at Margaret, but couldn't take his eyes off Pig Man.

"I'll be damned, Wolfe, it's him…"

"Our Father, who art in Heaven!" Margaret shouted with her arms outstretched to the sky. "Hallowed be thy name!" Pig Man approached her. Gazing at his little sister, like he was in hypnosis. "You remember this prayer, don't you brother?"

Sid stood up.

"What in the hell you doing, man? Stay down!"

"I can't anymore, D. I got to do my part."

He ran toward the house at an angle. He shifted himself in mid-air, reached across his body, and spun the throwing star toward Pig Man. It stuck him in the neck. Pig Man removed it, sniffed it, and dropped it to the ground like it was nothing but a pesky insect.

"See what they did to our brother!" Margaret said, pointing at Mills. "Look at him. *They* made you do that!" She picked at her eye. Then, with her index finger, pried her sunken eyeball out of the socket with her cracked nail. She tore the optical veins apart and admired her once decent eye before throwing it at Penny. It rolled for a moment and landed next to Wolfe's boot. A milky pupil, flecked with red, stared back at him. He crushed the eyeball into the ground with the tip of his boot. Unsalvageable.

Mills pulled the action back. "I told you to stay put!" He said it out of instinct, knowing he was going to pull the trigger. Samantha covered Penny's ears. She knew what was coming, too.

Deranged, Margaret stumbled from the porch and hobbled toward Penny. Mills pulled the trigger and put one right in her forehead. Her head snapped completely around to her left shoulder. Her brains exploded through the back of her skull. She fell to her knees and landed softly in a pool of her own blood.

Pig Man marched toward Mills.

"Wolfe, keep your goddam gun ready. This thing takes one more step..."

Wolfe didn't hesitate. He sprayed buckshot through Pig Man's overalls, causing him to wobble, but not fall. Wolfe regained his balance from the recoil and fired another shot. Another wobble.

Daryl felt the harmonica burning his skin through his

jeans. He removed it. An ochre glow surrounded it. He slowly made his way toward the others in a sleepwalking posture while Mills unloaded his entire clip on the Pig Man.

Once Daryl was a few feet away from them, a purple aura formed around Samantha, Penny, Wolfe, and Mills. It was the brightest color they had ever seen. They studied the surface, in awe at its beauty. Somehow, they all felt safe, like they were being protected by something not of this world.

Daryl peeled the balaclava over his face and put the harmonica to his lips. A sweet sound unlike any of them had ever heard before poured from it. The pigs dropped to the ground, as if in a lullaby. Pig Man dropped to his knees and shoved his stubby fingers into his mouth. His voice raspy, as he grunted and shook his head. He removed his fingers and began tearing away at his pointed ears, like they were suddenly a burden. He ripped them off and shoved them into his mouth, chomping away as he bellowed into the night air. Leaning up, he inserted his fingers into his snout and peeled his face in small spurts, cracking his head open and revealing his brain. Maggots crawled throughout its gray surface as it pulsed to the harmonica's rhythm.

The harmonica was now in complete control. Daryl became one with its magic, fully immersed in its power as it progressed methodically from one beautiful soft note to the next. He couldn't play these notes if he had a lifetime of practice, they were that amazing.

Pig Man stopped the commotion. His open skull pointed in Daryl's direction as the massive gray blob that was his brain danced about before finally exploding, covering the lawn of his family's farmhouse with dark plasma. The purple aura dissipated into a violet haze that hung there for the rest of the evening. Eventually it would vanish, along with Pig Man and his army of predatory swine.

"Is it over?" Penny asked Samantha, peeking at her through her fingers. "I couldn't watch."

Samantha brushed the hair out of Penny's face. "Yeah. It's over."

"What happened?" Penny said.

Wolfe removed his Stetson and ran his hand through his dark hair.

"Did you see that, Sheriff?"

Mills replaced his gun back in its holster.

"Sheriff?" Wolfe asked again.

Daryl's vision grew blurry. He began to sway, still drunk from the magic. That peaceful lullaby still lingered in his head like a good Springsteen song. Someone on the porch came into his focus before he fainted. It was the carnie from the county fair. The one who gave Daryl the harmonica for being 'Edlund's Strongest Man'. He was wearing Penny's blue-speckled hat and filing his nails, waving them in front of his mouth as he blew on them. He winked at Daryl, then vanished.

## LATER

Brad's funeral was nice. Closed casket. Everybody from that epic evening at the old farmhouse attended. Samantha cried for Penny. Penny cried because it was her Dad. Diana didn't cry at all. She was too medicated.

After her husband's murder (by Jud's shotgun), Diana sold

the country home in Edlund and she and Penny moved back to the city. The thought of starting over where they were supposed to be starting over to begin with seemed impossible. She got sober and started a blog called "Memoirs of a Grieving Wife" which got her a book deal (ironic since Brad was the writer of the two).

Penny fit in well at her new school and stayed in touch with Samantha through email and texts. Mostly texts.

SAMANTHA: Any cute boys in your class?

PENNY: Maybe.

SAMANTHA: *winking emoji*

Stuff like that.

Mills and Wolfe found a stick of dynamite on the ground after everyone left that night. They tossed it inside the farmhouse after dragging Jud and Margaret's body inside of it. There were a few explosions at first, but after that the house crumpled in a slow, quiet burn while fireworks exploded behind it. Nobody noticed that the house (or the cats) were destroyed. Mills thought that the violet haze had something to do with it. They never spoke about what happened. Occasionally they would exchange a glance whenever one of them would order bacon for breakfast. Which was always followed by an assuring "make that turkey bacon".

As for Daryl, Samantha, and Sid, they found themselves together once again on a perfect summer's day…

Samantha was updating her status on social media while Daryl snacked on a funnel cake. Thanks to laser technology, her face had minimal scarring. Not that that mattered. She was still the most beautiful girl Daryl had ever seen. The scars that were slightly present made her even more appealing.

They were proof that she was strong, a survivor. Sid was doing what he usually did, bobbing his head up and down to a conscious beat while he whispered to himself.

"Step right up! Test your strength! Come one, come all. Whether you're tall, medium, or small. Everyone has a chance to discover the wonder of The Great Mystery Box!"

That familiar voice grabbed Daryl's attention. He offered the funnel cake to Samantha, who put her hand on her stomach and made a sour face. Daryl dumped it in a nearby garbage can, as if to say "good riddance," and took Samantha by the hand.

"C'mon, Sam. This is the guy!"

"Who?"

"The guy I got the harmonica from!"

"He's awful loud. Maybe he has a microphone for Sid's rhymes!" She playfully punched Sid on his shoulder.

"It ain't the magic in the mic that brings the skills, Sammy. It's the MC."

Standing on a raised platform, the carnie puffed away at a small stogie below his pencil-thin mustache.

Outside of his purple silk shirt, he was dressed in all black: top hat, jacket, shoes, and slacks. An expensive upgrade from his second-hand wardrobe from before.

"Say there," the carnie said. "You look awful familiar to me, kid? Have we met?" He removed the cigar and poked it around in the air as he spoke.

"Ah yes! I do remember you. You're the harmonica player, right?"

"Yes sir," Daryl said. "I have it right..." he searched his

pockets for the harmonica, but it wasn't there. And he always kept it with him.

"I'm sure you do," the carnie said with a wink. "You'll find it again in due time, I'm almost sure of it."

"But, it was right..."

"Are we done here? Okay. You! Over there!" The carnie pointed at Samantha. "Come over here and give this a try, won't ya?"

"I don't think so. I'm not really into that sorta thing."

The carnie handed her a rubber mallet. "I won't take no for an answer, madam." He lowered his head, smiling. When he did, she could see something trying to come into focus from the reflection in his round sunglasses. "In fact, I insist."

"You better get up there, Sammy," Sid said. "He looks serious!"

The mallet was lighter than she expected. It looked much heavier. She raised it behind her head as it hung for just a moment in the bright sunlight before she sent it crashing down, crushing the red button and sending the metal puck toward a shiny bell. The machine lit up with neon lights. This was followed by a roar of applause which she found funny because there wasn't really anyone watching.

"We have a winner!" the carnie announced, turning his body and extending his hand, putting her on display like a good gameshow host does for its contestants.

He handed her The Great Mystery Box. She slid her hand into the blanketed hole and felt around where the side of the box should've been, but there didn't seem to be one. Something magnetized to her hand. It was warm and gave her a feeling of tremendous strength.

The carnie leaned into her.

"Go ahead and take it. You're going to need it."

**Thought Catalog**, it's a website.
www.thoughtcatalog.com

**Social**
facebook.com/thoughtcatalog
twitter.com/thoughtcatalog
tumblr.com/thoughtcatalog
instagram.com/thoughtcatalog

**Corporate**
www.thought.is

# About the Author

Sean Seebach is a husband, father, and restaurateur who has been publishing with Thought Catalog since June of 2015. Since then he has written many short stories involving various conjured devils including themes about morality, death, and hope.